FURY

FURY

FICTIONS AND FILMS

CLIVE HOLDEN

Cyclops Press

P.O. Box 2775, Winnipeg, MB, Canada, R3C 4B4

<www.cyclopspress.com>

Book design by Clint Hutzulak/Rayola Graphic Design

Photography by Clive Holden

(captured stills from the 16mm film Hitler!*)*

Printed In Canada.

First Printing February 14, 1998

ISBN 1-894177-00-2

The works included in this book are fictional,
and any similarity to real events, or persons living or dead,
is entirely coincidental, with the exception of
Gordon's Head and *Hitler! a filmpoem*
which have some autobiographical elements.

dedicated to my family

a portion of the proceeds from the sale of this book
will be donated to schizophrenic outreach and research

This book can be bought directly from
Cyclops Press via the Internet at:
www.cyclopspress.com
where samples from the film *Hitler!*
and the CD *Gordon's Head* & *Hitler!–experimental film soundtracks*
are also available.

Any enquiries may be sent to: mail@cyclopspress.com
or to the address on the front of this page.

FURY

a novella in 4

1

Jack Hammered All Day

4

JACKY FURY IN THE VANCOUVER DOCKYARDS,
JANUARY 13, 1969 AT 11 AM:

... Raining down his neck he worked a jackhammer that January on the harbour, prying up asphalt piece after piece, holding the hard metal body against his groin and lifting it with his right thigh, again his right thigh— his hard stomach his hard inner thigh—raining it's pooling in his boots and his hard steel toe, put it aside and shovel out the hole shoveling out the hole—the broken pieces of asphalt into the barrow pooling with rain, heaving again hard thighs lifting it up, up one, big, canine, tooth biting/biting/biting/biting life banging/hard against his groin it's raining in his pants today on the harbour, mooning blue white suds dancing, mean rain cool and tickling in his hairy groin, lifting his hard thing, lifting the long cold metal, colour of steel colour of rain—a manly voice says, 'Do that long enough you'll have muscles in your shit,' muscles in your shit, hard muscle on his thigh—lifting it up, rain along day, raining muscles, biting it-lifting it, it's dancing in his pants, it's his thing, the tight skin on his inner thigh, staining raining his industrial steel, his hard lifter, heaving it up, out and up, biting harder—it's raining down on him, in, into his open mouth, legs bent, weighted down, his groaning muscle, his hard loving hammer all day.

It was a few days

after Jacky's twentieth birthday he sailed from Dun Laoghaire to Liverpool, and from there to Montreal into the heart of America. He hitched and worked, hitched and worked right across to Vancouver in a few weeks and from there up north, where he got a job on a road crew on the Alaska Highway.

The rest of the crew decided he was a snob, because he read. One night they broke into his locker and took his books away, said he could only read *skin books* from then on. They made him sit with them night after night in the trailer bunkhouse while they drank Canadian Club and Skreech and played a game: two of them sat in chairs facing each other with their knees almost touching and flipped a coin, the loser held his hands behind his back. The winner wound up and punched the other full in the face, as hard as he could. The loser's head snapped back, the crack of bone on bone hung on the air. They switched then, back and forth, the final loser was the first to either fall off his chair, or flinch from a punch.

There was a postcard on the smoke-stained wall of a Mountie on horseback, with a cartoon balloon coming out of the horse's mouth that read: *Get This Asshole Off My Back!*

One night in that first north spring Jacky's body almost shook with the juice running in it. He stole the crummy and drove all the way to Whitehorse, a nine hour drive on the skinny, twisted oiled-dirt road, he didn't have a good reason, just to move, to feel the movement of earth under him and to see the world over the next hill. He finally parked on the main street in mid-morning, and on a whim he went into the barber and got his beard and long hair cut off. He went in looking like Sasquatch and came out fresh-cheeked and baby-faced.

Sitting in the Hotel having a fancy breakfast he read an ad in the Whitehorse Star: Coachways Bus Drivers Needed, Apply At Depot, which he could see out the window across the road.

You're just the kind of clean-cut young guy I've been waiting for, said Verne, the depot manager-janitor, and before Jacky knew it he was driving bus up and down the Alaska Highway, sleeping in towns with names like Cold River and Beaver Creek. He felt like an impostor. Like if people knew who he really was they'd fire him right away. But instead they gave him his own name plate to put above the windshield under the words: Safe, Reliable & Courteous.

The buses were freighters, the rear half for cargo with seats up front, he drove the spareboard three to four thousand miles a week on unpaved highway sprayed with crude oil, flat-out on the long alpine valley straightaways and then up and down another mountain top, suicide corners and mile long drops. Steamboat

Mountain had extra, hand-painted signs that said: Keep Right! Sound Horn! Dead Slow! in dripping red letters. The corners had no guard rails, a feeling on each that with a  flick of the wrist he could take off into space, it waited for him, huge and empty, the passengers asleep in back, trusting, not realizing what a thin line they were on.

At the top of Steamboat he'd stop at a dirt pull-off, usually in the middle of the night. A truck would come by once or twice an hour but it was mostly a peaceful, private place. There was a Christly cliff there, a mile high above a white, mirrored, snaking river. Pulling over to park with everyone asleep on-board, he'd close the door behind him and walk in back of the bus, stand at the edge of the cliff and piss off it into the black air. One night, after he'd lit a smoke and unzipped he looked up: two balls of fire hung huge and low over the peaks at the end of the black velvet valley, a blood-red sun just rising and a moon beside it, round, the same blood-red.

ONE OVER-NIGHT IN WATSON LAKE Jacky walked to the edge of town after last-call. There was a huge Texaco sign there, the tallest structure for hundreds of miles. He heard a buzzing noise that he thought was the drunk in his head until he looked straight up in amazement at the northern lights—he'd seen them once before from 'down south', from 'the outside'—the trucker who took him across Saskatchewan and Alberta pointed out the passenger window to a strip of hazy cloud following them on the north horizon, Jacky looked closer and it was actually a band of moving white light smeared onto the black canvas space. But up there the lights were right over his head and took up the whole sky, he lay down flat on his back on the gravel highway shoulder to watch: a green line, an orange and a pink one waving back and forth, crossing each other and stretching from one horizon to the other with an electric crackling like they were alive. He lay for a long time watching with his eyes wide trying to take in the whole of space, before he realized how it would look if someone from town saw him, the bus driver, flat on his back.

ALONG THE WAY he became known for his fast driving, and his drinking. He was good at both, but they were both starting to get him. The other drivers had accepted him when they saw he could keep the breakneck schedules, but there was no time to get acquainted, just enough to hand off the bus and tickets and then roar off further north or south. He was getting to be a binger, he could go weeks with just two or three beer to clear his head after work, but one day it would hit him, he'd drink like he was suffocating and the booze was  air. He'd lose hours at a time and wake up wondering what he'd done.

ONE NIGHT SOUTH OF TESLIN a group of young Indians stood having a party around a car in the middle of the highway, on a blind curve. Jacky saw them at the last second and slammed on the brakes, checked the wheel and fought going into a spin, he saw them turning slowly, looking calm as his highbeams bore down on them, they didn't move, they just stood there, frozen like totem deer. He skidded for two full bus lengths and came to a stop inches from them.

He got out yelling, What the Hell are you doing! but they just looked at him, quiet, a couple of them smiled until one young guy finally said, Been up pissing off the cliff again, eh?

JACKY MEMORIZED the road surface for over thirteen hundred miles from Dawson Creek to Dawson City, so he could drive as smooth as possible to not disturb his passengers. There were frost-heaves and huge holes that the front wheels slammed into if he wasn't on the ball, the whole bus would shudder and the wheel kick and try to pull out of his hands. But after a time he could avoid them, switching from one side of the road to the other the whole way—the locals were no problem but the few tourists or first-timers would get scared if he banged them around too much, Jacky could feel their eyes boring into the back of his neck, stiffening the muscles there like a fist.

That summer it rained for days, mud coating the sides of the bus up to the roof so the only place the passengers could see out was the windshield at the front. One dinner break they came to him in a posse of French, Germans and Americans and demanded he wash the windows, so they could *see*. He explained he didn't have time or tools but they demanded still that he wash them one by one with the gas pump squeegee if necessary, because they'd come up to *see* and they couldn't *see* anything.

HE WAS GETTING LONELY. One night on a lay-over he made love to an Indian woman in his motel room. What worried him the most after was that they hadn't used birth control. The woman, she said she lived in Calgary, was up north visiting her people.

There was a man in the bar that night, A hillbilly, from the black hills of Montana, he said, with his wife who was a Cherokee. Normally, Jacky had learned, prospectors in town after months in the bush needed to talk, not only to have a conversation, but to talk uninterrupted, sometimes for days. That night a table of people sat listening to the man from Montana with their mouths shut, nodding, his wife silent beside him, looking down at her lap. Jacky wondered if she ever got to talk. The man told them he communicated with nature in the woods, but it wasn't the same as talking to another human being.

Jacky was still in uniform, he didn't bother changing any more to go into a bar, he'd been up there long enough to realize no one cared and he could drink in public without raising eyebrows. He asked the hillbilly if he had a watch or a calendar in the woods. The man said, No, but I can tell you the time of day, or year, by the sounds in the brush, the different animals going up country and down, the birds.

Hours later at last call there were only the two of them at the table, Jacky and the hillbilly. The man's wife had slipped away an hour before as if she'd recognized something and didn't want to be part of it, she walked sideways a little with her head down.

Jacky realized how drunk he was only when he stood up to go to bed, but somehow then they were buying more beer and were headed for his room. In the hallway they met Gloria, a young Indian woman who they invited along, it was a party, it'd been a long time since anyone treated him so well.

But in the room the hillbilly started getting dark, or maybe it was Jacky's own eyes changing. The man from Montana started talking about guns, he asked Jacky if he had one, insisted he had to have a gun, A man's gotta be able to protect himself and his belongings! he said, from the way he was looking at the two of them, back and forth from Gloria to Jacky to Gloria, Jacky started to wonder vaguely if the man wanted some kind of threesome orgy, he'd read about them in the *skin* magazines. He heard the man talking about the war in South East Asia, ever since his return he wanted to live as far from people as he could get. But what the hillbilly said with his mouth and what he did with his eyes, they didn't seem connected any more, Gloria was becoming more and more the center of attention, the hillbilly going on about not trusting anybody, all the time watching her getting drunk too. Gloria, she was half nervous, half laughing at the two funny men.

Finally, the hillbilly from Montana decided: he looked at Jacky for a long time first, then at Gloria, then back at Jacky and no one spoke for a long time. The hillbilly said suddenly, This is no place for me any more tonight. His look was part wink at Jacky, and part, I-just-might-pull-out-my-gun-and-kill-you-right-now. Then he left.

After a couple of minutes Gloria wanted to go too and she said, I'd better be going. But Jacky wanted to make love. He had only done it twice before. What he really  wanted was to hold her body in his arms. He was sitting between her and the door and as she stepped towards it he held out his arm, partly to talk with but partly to bar her way, Please, stay, with me tonight, he whispered, barely aloud. What he felt was, I haven't even touched another human being in over a year. But what he finally said to her was, Aw, c'mon, stay a while. Then came more pleading, cajoling, and more barring her way.

Gloria looked at him. She was tempted because he was pretty. But she shouldn't. On the other hand she was tired, and sometimes it's just easier to say yes. All right, she said. She was standing in front of his chair as he put his arms around her legs and pressed his face against the lap of her jeans.

They got undressed while Jacky worried dimly he had no condom but he didn't say anything, he was afraid she'd change her mind if he somehow broke the spell. On the bed he didn't know what to do so he asked her to go on top and she nodded and straddled him. He didn't know that she needed to be held as much as he did, or about waiting for her to moisten, or that the two were at all connected. She guided him with her hand, and like the times before he was surprised at the angle it took inside of her, he was all the way inside her, but she was still dry and in pain.

I haven't been with a man for a long time, she said quietly. I'm sorry, this hurts, could we do it lying down?

He nodded and she came off and lay on her back. She saw how awkward he was and helped guide his body over hers. Like with the others it wasn't like they looked in magazines. He was too ashamed to ask her for help. She took hold of him again and guided him inside, he was lying on her and afraid of crushing her, he had no idea what to do with his arms or legs, so she tried to teach him. Then, slowly, they started a light rocking movement forward and back rolling on her hips, there was a delicious light rubbing and for a few moments they rocked, very gently. She moaned and he was really hard and beginning to understand. Then he came.

He rolled off of her. He suddenly worried he might have started another human being inside her. And he hadn't kissed her.

He fell into a black sleep, holding her tight.

But she wasn't there when he woke up. He never saw her again.

THE NEXT NIGHT, it was about 2 am, Jacky crossed the little steel bridge south of Toad River. He must have blinked. He hit the bridge doing seventy five miles an hour, at the other end he knew, *he knew* it dipped down into the dark and there was a hair pin, a huge yellow and black checkered sign with a bent-over arrow and 20 MPH marked it but he forgot what he was doing or where he was—he must have lost concentration for a

just a second, it seemed like waking up from a dream just as the front wheels hit the road surface at the far end of the bridge with everything in slow motion—he saw the big sign ahead in his lights still going full highway speed, his foot starting to move through the heavy sand of space, reaching—and finally hitting the brakes. The nose of the bus dove down just as he had to crank the wheel hard, the tires bit in and locked, there was so much weight with the freight in the back piled to the roof he'd always been afraid it would break loose and come around one day and the passengers mostly sleeping were thrown ahead yelling or sucking-in breath. It all happened in a few seconds. Jacky let up on the brakes and the wheels tried to hold on, they rounded the corner on the last part of the shoulder, a wheel nibbling at the edge of nothing just shy of heading down into the river. The rapids there. Jacky had seen them other nights. White manes leaping on oil-black water.

If he'd day-dreamed for one more second he'd have killed them all, but no one said a thing, they went back to sleep after awhile. Maybe it was an animal, he heard someone say. He kept on driving, he couldn't let them see his inner shaking, his nerves, he had to keep on tunneling into the dark.

THE NEXT DAY in his hotel room Jacky woke really sick. He phoned Verne who swore at him because he'd have to double-shift the other driver which wasn't very legal, you just weren't supposed to be sick. But he was sweating full-on with his sheets soaked through and then shivering cold and shaking like a new leaf in a stiff breeze. Through the afternoon his throat slowly closed so he could barely swallow, he didn't move from his bed for three days. He thought he was dying.

Finally they found him in there, a maid ignoring the Do Not Disturb sign told the desk and they bundled him into a taxi and took him to hospital, where he was out for two more days and woke with a plastic tube in his arm. A nurse, a young Indian girl came in and asked meekly if he felt O.K., she said he'd had strep throat and rheumatic fever when they brought him in with a temperature of a hundred and five. He couldn't answer her. He thought she was Gloria.

He quit, he got the Hell out of there.

2

Power
Authority

JULES LE GRAND IN A CONDO
OVERLOOKING PLATEAU MONTRÉAL,
FEBRUARY 3, 1999 AT 2:02 AM:

... *When they got going, he felt that half crazy—it'd been almost two
weeks, first her period and then he had a herpes, then she had one, plus a
couple of days for good measure while he was tired, or she didn't feel like it,
the tension building and both of them thinking maybe that was it, maybe it
was over—then, they found a way back in, he came into the living room
and she wasn't there, there was a pile of blankets on the couch and he
thought, maybe, it didn't look like it, but he poked with his finger anyway
and she was in there, it shocked him, it really looked like she wasn't there—
he opened a corner and stuck his head inside with her, her face was so sweet
and sexy in the dim light, her neck so soft, he bit lightly on her nipple
through her shirt and she moaned very quietly, her bare legs moved a little
and he put his arm between them, flexing it upwards and pressing his muscle
against her—when he kissed her on the mouth she bit his lip hard and
moved her tongue on his teeth and against his tongue, her hands went under
his shirt and she clawed softly at his chest, her back arching, all still under
the blankets—he came out into in the red light from the Christmas rubber*

20

plant they'd decorated together and refused to take down, while she stayed under the blankets from the waist up, her thighs milky red, her skin velvet warm—he kissed inside her legs, opening her, he started to lick her and she said, Be careful, and he realized he hadn't shaved in three days, so he stretched his tongue as far as he could—he didn't want to go inside yet, because he wouldn't last long—in her muffled voice she moaned and from deep in the blankets she said, Put on a condom, so he did—wrapping her legs around his waist he lifted her off the couch the blankets falling away, her breasts were round and full in the warm light her arms were around his neck and he was far away deep inside her, she let out a sharp cry, but he didn't want to come yet so he came out again, lay her down and put two fingers inside, he moved them hardly at all—she grabbed fistfuls of his hair as he licked her gently, like a bird walking on new snow without falling through, he pushed his fingers in a little harder and she howled long and loud like he'd never heard before and he was on top and inside her and she cried and he shot straight up to her heart—and it was okay again, for awhile.

The expropriation

went through when Jules was nine. It was to make way for the new, monster-sized aeroport mirabel. Maman and Pops refused to go. Until the Mounted Police came and removed them physically, by force.

The government took five times the amount of land they needed, they said they'd build a new city with work for one hundred thousand people. But it never happened. The family moved to a brand new house in St. Guy, thirty miles south just above the river from Montreal. It was mainly farms and forest then. The house had one long slanting roof with dirt lawns and muddy blacktop in front and a *carport*.

Rue de Bellevue was one of the new roads, it bent gracefully like the neck of a swan, its surface hard and smooth. One day Jules and Giselle from up the street lay down on the road on their sides, ten yards apart. They rolled a softball back and forth to each other. Jules watched it roll towards him growing bigger and bigger until he stopped it with his hand in front of his face— and then it became smaller and smaller when he rolled it away, back towards her.

ONE NIGHT, when they were building the aeroport, Jules rode his bike all the way up, two hours one way. He ripped out hundreds of surveyor's stakes, poured sand into bulldozer fuel tanks, smashed flood lights and spray-painted swear words on the vacant terminal walls.

The old farm house sat empty for years. Jules camped in it, hiding from the RCMP and the Sûrcté Privée until one day he went up with Marie-Claude from biology class and a case of beer. Hydro Québec had knocked it down, they were erecting a five-storey transmission tower over the exposed cellar.

Sometimes Jules went up to the aeroport after a yelling match between Maman and his father. Pops was drinking away the expropriation money as fast as he could.

ON THE FIRST WARM DAY in April Jules sat on the edge of the Lac des Deux Montagnes below the Oka Monastery with Manon who worked in her grandparents' dépanneur, she was already wearing shorts and an orange halter top with no bra. She had big breasts for her age and Jules couldn't help looking, but she seemed to like it. The lake was still frozen white, he liked all the space there, it made his head feel better.

There was a movement up the shore, at first they couldn't make it out, but then they saw it was a large black swan sitting and watching out like them. It stood  awkwardly and walked slowly towards them. Manon said maybe it escaped from one of the rich houses up-river.

The black bird inspected the shore as it came, nosing in the bushes and half-thawed garbage while Jules and Manon sat still, holding their breath and waiting. Finally it sat just out of their reach, looking out across the lake again. They stared at its smooth, waxy feathers, its brick-red bill and eyes, and after some time it stood again, took a few more clumsy steps and sat right at their feet as if asking to be touched. They were afraid to scare it away, to break the spell, but carefully slowly Jules reached out and lightly stroked the feathers on its back, once, pulling his hand away. He was surprised its feathers were so hard and strong. And it stayed with them. They both reached out and brushed its wings, Jules moved closer and put his hand full on its back, he could feel its heart beating inside. The bird wasn't fragile at all like he expected, he reached out and stroked its long, thick, dark neck, it was hard, tight muscle inside, that straightened when he touched it and then curved slowly, back into his hand.

HE WAS ON THE BUS coming home from a trip to the city back across Jesus Island past brick and white stucco houses rippling red snow fences and giant shopping malls with bright plastic signs coloured like huge children's toys. As he watched he could feel the lightness growing inside him as everything shifted and lay over everything else—the patterns of light inside sliding over the seats, the floor and the people sitting.

He stepped off the bus in front of the school. As it pulled away it was like a curtain drawing open: it was all there the lines all the light the road the bright new Petro Canada station and the sky, the right colours and the people standing working or in their cars, attached to it all without knowing. He'd been to the same place in his head before, a few times, but always by accident.

Just before Jules was kicked out of school he painted a picture in art class of the Petro Can station, the light was from a late afternoon in winter the lit signs' black and blood-red falling and staining the drifts and icy blacktop. Along the horizon was a strip of silver light that was often there on that kind of day, south, above the city. The more he painted the more his eyes seemed to change, he worked for hours at lunch and after school and he started to find that special place every day, *but on purpose*. He'd start to paint, and it was like the bus was pulling away, *he could see*.

When he tried to talk about it with his friends they laughed and said he was stoned. But he didn't usually toke with them. It was too much, like getting pushed the last inch off a cliff. He worked on the gas station painting for weeks. People saw it from the hallway and came in, they liked it, it was his last painting.

JULES HAD AN ANCIENT, beat-up Parisienne he'd bought off a neighbour for 50 bucks as soon as he was old enough to drive. One day at lunch hour he was driving it through downtown St. Guy, there was a traffic jam ahead and he joined in the honking. Until he saw the trouble was someone who'd fallen in the road. It was a drunk. It was Pops. Jules sat watching as their neighbour got out of his car at the front of the line and helped his father to the curb. Jules did a U-turn and floored it the other way.

Later that day he was expelled, for telling the principal to, *Go fuck yourself*. He wanted to know why Jules missed so many classes. Jules told him to, *Suck my dick*. Then he was out.

He drove hundreds of miles that night flat-out in the dark and pounding rain, first circling the outskirts of the city and then up and down the St. Laurent. Near Trois Rivières he sat looking out over the river wondering what would happen next? He ended up at mirabel again. He still went up but not as often, always at night to cause a little trouble if he could. That night he lay in the rain-soaked grass and sawed for hours through a huge bolt in the leg of a light tower beyond the main runway, he'd been working on it for years, sawing in different places and lying pressed flat when the planes took off and landed. He stood and picked up the huge old axe he'd found in the old cellar and started swinging at the bolt. He tried to make big clean circles with the axe in the air like he remembered his father doing, it made a dull clank and shuddered up his arms each time he hit the great impassive girder. His grandfather had used the same axe in the woods in winter when the ice roads were open and you could walk anywhere. *Like goddamned Jesus in a toque*, he'd said. Jules made high circles in the air over his head with all his back and both arms bringing the old axe down, each time jarring to a clanging stop on the bolt, sparks in the dark. He forgot himself and had to dive flat at the last minute covering his ears as a jumbo descended overtop of him its roar filling every space and then gone as quickly off towards the terminal, wheels screaming on impact and engines rising to a fever pitch as it touched-down a half mile away.

He was about to give up when the tower suddenly creaked and let out a deep moan over his head. Before he could react a huge metal leg twisted sideways like a dinosaur bending its knee, the tower swayed slightly to one side but stopped. He scrambled to his feet as another leg snapped clean-through and the whole tower came crashing down towards him, the massive girders groaning like extinct monsters as he ran. He leapt face down into a choked ditch as it thundered onto the ground.

Jules ran as fast as he could across the same dark grass fields his great-grandparents had plowed back to his car in a ravine. The principal had yelled after him as

he went out the office door, *If you can't get along here in school, you won't get by in the real world!*

A few days later he applied for work at the Commonwealth Veneer Company in St. Guy. He told the man in the white shirt that he wasn't afraid of hard work. Jules saw it, the man wrote *Good Attitude* at the top of his application form.

WHEN HE FIRST SAW WENDY she worked in one of those restaurants that serve extra-big sandwiches to tourists in the city, she worked the cash, she had to spin around and around in one spot, facing the long line of customers to take their money, joke and poke fun—she laughed, spinning, made coffee, poured a drink, spinning, made fun of a man's stupid hat, spinning, spinning.

She was two years older than Jules, with jet-black hair, real red lips, a face with more warmth in it, more room telling him to, *Hey, climb on in here,* it said. *There's a whole universe of room in here for you to be loved in. What, shy? Hey, nice little ass you've got there, and eyelashes, the longest I've ever* seen on a man—*you look a little straight, but no, there's something lean and strange about you—you like my hips? Breasts? Think you could handle it?* She wore black clothes with a bit of red, she took his money, spinning away, but turning for an instant to glance up into his face, he looked right back, it was her he wanted.

He sat at a table, she knew he was staring at her, he couldn't help it, she glanced over her shoulder now and then, trying to size him up and spinning away again. American tourists lined up to eat the thick meat sandwiches, *To shit them out later*, thought Jules, *They look like cattle themselves.* There was rocking music in her hand that rested on her hip as she bent back twisting away from another customer and looking directly at Jules who looked right back, in her eyes there was challenge, warmth, heat, steel and muscle and his long boned hands that wanted to grab her tight below her ribs. She spun back, but not before a glimpse of another seriousness in her eyes: her trying to decide if he was worth anything, or if he was just another idiot. She thought maybe he wasn't.

Jules had a swirling sensation—but he left without talking to her.

He was afraid.

IT WAS YEARS LATER when he saw her again, at a Christmas party in Old Montreal. Jules was *slaqué* at the mill, collecting Unemployment Insurance. He liked to drive into  the city and go for walks all over late at night. He was wandering through the narrow cobble-stoned streets near the Hôtel de Ville when he heard noise from the party and just went in, no one stopped him. In fact, no one seemed to see him even though he towered over most of them. He had a beer and was getting bored when he almost knocked her over in the kitchen doorway, she looked at him like he was a ghost, but a welcome one. He made sure to talk to her this time, or to let her talk, she told him she worked for a TV station.

JULES AND WENDY WERE TOGETHER for eleven weeks. On their last night, they got home after a concert, they'd had a lot to drink and Jules couldn't make love, he said he just wanted to go to sleep and he lay beside her on the bed when Wendy started to cry. She lied it had nothing to do with him. She couldn't stop though. She curled into a ball facing the wall, her back shaking with sobs. Jules didn't know what to do, he sat beside her feeling useless, he couldn't sleep so he started to read the paper that was on the floor beside the bed, which made her angry, she swiped it out of his hand swearing at him, and lay there crying until after the sun came up.

That morning, when she finally fell asleep he left her condo for the last time.

HE TOOK A TINY ROOM on rue St. Dominique a few blocks from her building, he didn't like to spend time in St. Guy any more. For three months he sat in there hunched on an old kitchen chair, staring out the window at the tiny parking lot across the narrow street, *Pigeon Square*, he called it, where dozens of filthy birds nodded and talked quiet all day with a low rolling sound in their throats like water in a pool—until someone disturbed them and they swooped up in one movement like they were connected, their wings flashing lightdarklight in seconds flowing out over the Café Portuguais, each time rounding the same invisible bend in the air and then down again over the parking lot— they always stopped and hovered, in the same rhythm, before landing. Every now and then the pigeons were sent into flight by a customer exiting the back of the Cinéma L'Amour, the door opening and a man appearing with his shoulders pulled up and forward ready to walk quickly away—but as he stepped onto the asphalt a hundred birds would fly in his face, the beat of their wings like drums in his ears.

Jules would have gone in too if he thought it would do him any good. But those kind of films had never done it for him, the acting and writing were so bad, he could  never get off, or even get into the story. He seemed to need a story. And he thought of the actresses, it was depressing.

Suddenly it was spring. Jules woke up late one day, his room was hot and winter was over, he pushed the window wide and the snow was melted and almost gone, there were a few small drifts left and puddles running on the wet pavement with steam rising into the sunshine, everything smelled of wet growth sweet and rude, the uncovered dog turds against the back wall of the grocery and the moist scent of the naked park two blocks away. The Portuguese men all came out to stand on the corner, laughing and saying things only they understood at the young women walking by swinging their arms lightly, suddenly in thin cotton dresses and little else.

The temperatures soared and one stinking hot day a yellow stillness grew in the air, the city was hushed, when sounds did reach Jules they were muffled and distant like someone yelling in a far away, locked room. He watched people hurrying outside—they looked confused and kept to themselves. It quickly grew dark, black clouds crowded over the city and it started to rain, hard right away, a wall of water crashing down onto Montreal. Thunder exploded right outside the window and Jules heard himself yelling in time with it, staring out wide-eyed as avenue Duluth filled with water, explosions shaking the little brick building over and over while his excitement rose. He loved thunder. It was how he felt, he moved his arms wide in time with the claps, he was making it happen, him—in minutes a violent river roared down off the mountain coursing through the street below.

He heard it on the radio later, in the flash-flood a truck driver drowned when his trailer was submerged in an expressway tunnel. A businessman was killed instantly by lightning, walking by the downtown cafés on Crescent St. Jules felt guilty. Like it was his fault.

He sat in that window staring out at the light shifting and the people walking by. He couldn't think of anything else he wanted to do.

Then there was a re-call at the mill.

BEFORE HE STARTED at the Commonwealth Veneer Company his hands were soft, *Like an artist's*, Maman said. Now they were covered in scars and thin lines of dried blood. The re-call was temporary, they were shutting down for good and wanted them on three shifts, seven days, until they cleared out the old stock. He got his vintage 1973 Firebird TransAm out of the garage where he stored it for the winter. It had 199,000 miles on it and still didn't rattle. Its only problem was sometimes you turned the key and all that happened was a loud *click*—he had to get out and poke at the starter  motor with a broom handle and try again. This always worked though. He knew he should buy a new starter, but he liked shrugging and saying to people as he opened the hood, *Hey, reste tranquille, there's no panic.* He drove it in big circuits around and around St. Guy before his first evening shift back, he exited the autoroute, gearing down, the car's huge engine bucking the ramp like a rodeo horse, he meant to check at the new Canadian Tire Store in the Centre Bon Marché to see if they had the starter motor but the lot was empty, closed for the holiday. He forgot it was Canada Day, in the windows Happy Canada Day posters competed for space with Bonne Fête de la St. Jean Baptiste from the week before, red and white maple leafs and blue and the white fleur-de-lis. In St. Guy some celebrated one day and some the other. In his family they had celebrated both, plus the fourth of July, Grandmother La Grande had grown up MacDiarmid in Dorval, and Maman was part Mexican-American, her grandparents met crop picking in Maine. But after the aeroport the family threw out all their flags.

In the years since his family arrived St. Guy had become another huge suburb, Jules drove down the shrub-lined streets counting the space-vans, econo-compacts, boats on trailers and campers on pick-ups, everything new and clean but with soft edges, mowed grass and summer flowers, the houses *ranch-style* but boxier with bricks and stucco mixed, Québec and California. On the news they called St. Guy a *bedroom community*, like no one really lived there, they only slept for eight hours and went back to their real lives in the city. The fields where he'd played as a teenager were being covered with quiet, curving, designed roads and the politicians were promising a fast train to the city.

An old Eric Clapton tune was on the radio, *A real classic*, the D.J. called it as Jules turned off boulevard St. Guy and pulled up in front of the house. The boulevard was one of the older roads in St. Guy that followed the original flow of the river and the shape of the land, or ran straight where it used to border a farm. Maman still lived there on the corner of Rue de Bellevue beside the last field and woods in St. Guy between the river and the road—as he got out of the car he noticed the giant yellow bulldozer sitting silent in the centre of the field.

Maman called through the door to come in but hardly looked up when he entered the living room, she didn't have much to say to anyone any more. He watched The Price Is Right with her. She'd never lock the door, no matter how many times he asked her, like she was still on the farm. Jules didn't know what he was doing there, so he left.

Outside, he walked across the old field. Along the river they'd already pushed over most of the sycamores and old Empire apples, the CAT sat like a big dumb bully ready to finish tearing into them the next day.

There was a sign at the edge of the field with a map announcing the future Club de Golf de St. Guy.

JULES, 'EH JULES! his partner yelled in the stamp and howl of the machine—they started flipping veneer again one after another never running out of the thin sheets of wood dropped in waist high stacks by a two storey fork lift—they each took hold of a side, checking for knots or tears and lifting, flipping it quick like a stiff bed sheet in the air while they made three steps to the machine, they were extensions of it, feeding it all day and night— the veneer fell with a wood-on-metal *thunk*, then the core, ply scraps soaked in glue spitting out of rollers *phtt-pht-pht-t-t-t-t-t* landing against the grain, the dark layers in a piece of plywood—a pair of hands sent them through from the other side, Jules didn't know Paulo too well, he worked five feet from him all shift but he was always surrounded by machine, he saw the rest of him only for a second when the alarm rang out that meant he was out of core, the alarm grinding and it was Jules' job to walk around the machine bowing his back to move up the next horse-high cart—usually there was a song in his head, whatever played last on his car radio before work, tonight it was a crashing beat and a woman singing, *I need a man!* He remembered the singer

from the video channel in the taverne her long white-
blonde hair and thick puckered lips moving toward and
away from the glass screen and the rocking wide curves
of her shiny dress, the slow and heavy rock beats helped
the most, the songs were something there to keep his
arms and legs doing the right things in the right
order—but he had to be careful not to hear some
advertising jingle, it would play in his head the whole
shift and he'd make mistakes, dropping things and never
getting into the rhythm, even with a good song he had
to be careful not to drift completely away, he had to
keep one foot there on the floor of the mill—they
brought back the rhythm, three steps back / lift a sheet
/ three steps ahead / flipping it down into the press,
wiping with the back of his arm at the sweat on his
forehead, slipping goggles, wet elastic and rubber
gloves, face and arms painted in itchy, sweet-smelling,
sawdust and glue, if they went fast enough
stepping/lifting/dropping for about an hour to get
ahead of the machine a different alarm rang and there
was a five minute break—they sat then while the
machine caught up and the sweat from his armpits
cooled and rippled down his stomach into his pants,
they said nothing, they had to yell to be heard, the taste
of salt and wood—then back to it and faster and faster
again until the right speed, that they could keep up and
just keep going for maybe another hour until the alarm
stopped the machine again—when he had the beat he
only needed a thumb and one finger on each hand to
suggest where the sheet should go—they took three

more steps, but at that second when the veneer hung on the air and weighed nothing, he felt something snap deep inside his wrist the grip suddenly leaving his  fingers the music in his head stopping and a sheet falling crossways, jamming the machine.

The slowest clock in the world sat high and silent on a wooden beam overhead. Jules held his wrist, moving it back and forth, an advertising jingle started in his head as an alarm rang out in the reverberation of the mill.

ÇA VA, SEEMS O.K. TO ME, said the attendant in the First Aid Room digging into Jules' wrist with both his thumbs. Jules didn't feel pain any longer and his fingers moved fine again, the truth was he felt excited, it welled up from deep inside him like a good secret but he couldn't let anyone see. He watched the First Aid man's TV set, the pretty coloured images flickering by one after another when an ad came on for the Late News, Wendy reading the headlines, her face serious then friendly, concerned then inviting, *Details tonight...* her hair was a careful arrangement of dark flames, the attendant laughed at the look on Jules' face, *What the hell,* he said. *Why don't you take the rest of the shift off.*

Jules had thrown out his TV but he still saw her on bus shelter ads, on a billboard beside the bridge to the city and sometimes just floating in the air in front of him, naked, her arms and legs open saying to him, *Welcome home, this is your home.* The excitement that had been rising in him all day was gone as he stepped back into the smells, heat and noise of the mill, he looked up at the corrugated metal roof high overhead. He had no idea whether it was light or dark, wet or dry outside. He didn't care. After all, he'd made some overtime working the holiday. The song from an ad for a chain of drug stores played in his head, the store's name sung over and over to a famous Italian opera.

40

OUTSIDE THE MILL the night air was sweet and heavy in his nostrils, he walked through the bay where people from the city backed their cars for fake firewood pressed from the mill's sawdust waste, the Presto factory was a tin building stuck onto the side of the mill with a huge old machine like a steam locomotive inside filling the space to the roof with giant iron wheels, long roving arms and timed bursts of steam ending in a short conveyor belt—the machine chugged out round logs like foot-long rabbit turds, half-a-dozen senior men boxed them and joked about working at *le trou de cul*, the asshole of the mill.

There was a sign beside the main gate that read: 99 Jours sans un Accident—99 Days Without an Accident. Jules checked his watch, waited, and right on time there  was thudding hard thunder from not far north, sharp like a metal hand clap and then a deep roll—a second's delay and a current in the ground rumbled under him, up through his legs and out his arms while the lights of the mill, the parking lot, and the autoroute flashed once and went to black.

During a long, blind second the high drone of the machines in the mill dropped in pitch and stopped. There was a lone, distant car horn and the men's voices started inside, mixing with the frogs ratcheting on the banks of the Thousand Islands River, Jules felt free with the white starkness of the stars stretched above him over the breathing velvet-blackness all around.

THE POWER WAS ONLY OFF for half an hour but most of the shift was in the Taverne TV-Rock-Vidéo-Shooters et Plus by then. Jules sat with his partner from the glue spreader who was built like a decathlete, he called him Bruce for Bruce Jenner, he was a pure Anglo from Cornwall, Ontario, was hired the same year as Jules and was the same age but had three kids at home and another one on the way. Two of the older guys sat with them at one of the little round tables with faded-red terri-towel covers held on by elastic underneath. They switched to *franglais* because they liked Bruce, a mix of English with French thrown in the holes where the words didn't come quickly enough. *Seize, sixteen?* asked the big waitress, Jules nodded, staring ahead with his mouth open waiting for the beer. A minute later she was back, her round tray full with glasses, her hand flew as she transferred them to the table until its surface was covered and they did what they did after every shift, they each reached for a glass and drank it down in one long breath, they reached for another, drank the first half down and then the second right away, they reached for a third glass and it wasn't until then that they relaxed into their chairs and took a look around the room for the first time, shaking their heads as they started to clear, they crossed their legs with one ankle resting on the other knee, settled into their bodies and examined the soles of their boots. In his pocket Jules had a copy of the Commonwealth Veneer Company Limited's annual report. The company had grown to the point where wood products were only one of the things they were doing around the world. The report had colour photos of computers, household cleaning liquids and other products they made or sold and lists of real estate holdings including their new pink granite headquarters on blvd. René Lévesque. Not everyone was surprised about the shut-down, the union had given big concessions and turned a blind eye to safety because the

company promised they'd build a new particle board plant fifty kilometers north and hire on people from St. Guy first choice. Instead they were building one in
North Carolina, *And I heard one in Mexico*, said Bruce. Jules had visited the company's headquarters, the luxurious lobby, chandeliers, fountains, tropical plants and a grand piano, he sat on a leather couch for awhile watching the suits go by.

They'd been there five minutes, finishing their fourth beers and from over his shoulder, *Seize!?* Someone said, *Oui*, and Bruce Jenner turned to him, *So, when you gonna sell me that piece-a-shit you call a car? I'll give you a hundred bucks for it.* A preview of the Late News started on the movie-sized TV screen beside them, a giant Wendy suddenly appearing mouthing words silently with a stern expression, there was a photo of a power transmission tower behind her head with a little time-bomb logo over it, up-close she was shadow blurs of red, white and creamy pink, her lips moving in and out, her eyes sparkling like bottle glass. They all turned in their seats to watch.

LATER, JULES WAS PART of the high speed stream of traffic on the autoroute that still coursed in towards the city's late night holiday attractions. On the radio a song ended and the FM announcer spoke in a deep voice, *No word as yet on who or what group blew up a transmission tower north of Montreal tonight causing a massive but temporary power failure. Hydro Québec is asking everyone to turn off their air conditioners for tonight, they say the grid is 'slightly impaired' and there may be further problems if they can't borrow enough from Ontario or the states while repairs are under way.* Jules felt light inside, as if the drive was blowing the old, stale air out of his mind. *Black Dog* by Led Zeppelin started and he turned it up as thunder sounded from not far off. When he'd left St. Guy the sky had flashed yellow-white over Vermont, and as he crossed Laval the storm spread towards the downtown, making a silhouette of Mount Royal—on the summit, the electric white crucifix glowed beside broadcast antennae in the shape of a red pitchfork. Another clap sounded like dynamite right over his car and he sped up as it started to rain, lightly for a second and then he was forced to slow as the autoroute was suddenly covered in sheets of water, all he could see were distorted red tail lights ahead and white fish eye reflectors that marked the lanes, he liked it, it was like a good video game, he sped up again passing slow cars weaving in and out. Sometimes the alarms from work sounded in his head and they wouldn't stop for days.

44

THE RAIN WAS OVER by the time he got out of his car in the downtown, he stood watching the holiday crowd on the St. Catherine strip, the slick road  surface swam with electric blue, yellow and red, steam rose bleeding colours into the air and high above the cold white-lit towers of the business sector loomed over the city's centre, empty banks, insurance, timber and mining companies and the Hydro Québec building in the centre with its logo, a giant glowing Q with lightning for a tail.

Jules heard a long scream and turned to see it came from a speaker over an appliance store window, it was the high whine of a black Italian sports car on three banks of TVs, a young male model driving down a winding country road / a close-up of his grip on the gearshift moving through four gears / the numbers one-two-three-four flashing / him pulling on a tight leather glove one finger at a time / his blank face, cool, ready / the square back of the car pulling away from the camera / in a corner of the screen a box of condoms, and the words: *four packs-for you-for your love.*

As he watched, the TVs suddenly blinked off and everything was black, for just a second, then the street-lights, neon and office towers suddenly appeared again, the sets and lights flickering several times, a teenage girl's excited scream and several young men in different directions yelling and whooping like they were at a rock concert. The whole downtown had disappeared and reappeared before anyone could move. The power stayed on. Jules remembered telling Wendy, stupidly, that she should quit her job, that he didn't like her being on the TV.

Normally in the city he had to fight off all the yelling signs, the tall buildings in close groups, the people dressed to be seen and not to blend in and the cars weaving head-to-ass through it all in a coloured metal river, sometimes it was too much at once crowding him inside his head. But this time was new, he felt a thick black cloud in his guts, like smoke rising, it felt good, there was space enough to do whatever he wanted. And he wanted to hit something as hard as he could. He walked faster, people got out of his way, he circled through the downtown neighbourhoods randomly choosing one street or another, deciding which way to go at each intersection. He felt a new, dark power that drove him on—he was glad to feel anything for a change.

An hour later on a circuit across the Plateau he stopped, realizing he was below a second floor bar he knew. He'd found it when it was an empty Portuguese pool hall, he'd kept coming over the years even after it was discovered and became jammed with young art students watching each other, feeling their own power in the music that pounded the room like an earthquake. Jules' black shadow followed him up the stairs like a stain moving on the wall and he slipped into the sound, smoke and crush of young bodies.

He sat in a corner with a quart bottle of O'Keefe's in his hand and his legs spread wide. Les Canadiens were playing exhibition with the Russians on the old  Motorola above him but he couldn't get into it, the players skated around, bumping into each other like insects flying around a light bulb. Really, what he *really* felt like doing was picking up the table and throwing it through the window, following it out himself, falling into the empty—his fingers gripped the table edge, his knuckles turning white and his arm muscles tightening, but he could never actually do it.

At a table across the room there was a young man in a V-neck sweater, dressed *ivy league*, like he was on a rowing team. His date had carefully set blonde curls, like a sorority queen in a fifties teen movie. They were out of place there, thought Jules, like him, but for different reasons. It was almost six months since he'd brought Wendy there, he remembered holding her, sure the sex too, but holding her all night long, he could still feel her on the palms of his hands, her wide white hips and the lily-soft skin on her belly. His open hand suddenly slammed down onto the table top, startling himself and everyone around him. He saw the older punk waitress point him out to the owner, nodding in his direction and looking right at him, the owner was an ex-wrestler, there was a black and white photo on the wall of him wearing the silver and leather championship belt, his stomach was smaller then. His big voice suddenly yelled over the deafening music at two young men who were dancing too close, they scowled and pulled apart. If Jules thought about her for too long he ended up hitting something. Sometimes, in the Taverne in the middle of a friendly conversation, his fist would slam down making everyone jump. They'd look at him like they'd never really known him before.

The college boy was searching frantically for something, he couldn't find his wallet, the waitress' gray crew cut and studied blank face stood over them waiting. She'd found a place where the tips were good, she could dress the way she liked and none of the kids would dare touch her. She walked away calmly with the beers still high on her tray, winding effortlessly across the packed dance floor. After a while the V-neck gave up searching his pockets and the floor and started to scan the crowd, angry and determined. His gaze fell onto two young Portuguese from the neighbourhood at a table close by. They were almost his age, dressed in work clothes, in the bar where their fathers and older brothers drank before the neighbourhood had changed. They watched the game and pretended it was still their place. The rower stared hard at them for a long time, Jules could see his gears turning, deciding: *One of them took my wallet.* The college boy stood and leaned on their table with his arms out straight like a cop on TV. It was an interrogation, the rower was putting on a show for the lady. The two young Portuguese didn't seem to mind at all, they just shrugged and stood, raised their arms high and pulled their pockets inside out as he frisked them.

They've done this before, thought
Jules, they grew up downtown and
it was easier to go along, until the
rower gave up and went away—
and anyway, his father had more
money than theirs. The rower slumped dejectedly back
to his table, the two young Portuguese taking up watching the game again like nothing had happened.

But the young man wouldn't give up. His eyes finally
came to rest on Jules away in his corner who stared back
at him, his eyes begging him to, *C'mon, try it with me.*
Again, Jules could see him decide: *It was that guy sitting in
the corner who took my wallet.* They sat for a long time
looking at each other across the room while Jules drank
his beer and hoped.

Finally, the rower got up and walked to the bar where
the waitress waited. He pointed at Jules but she shrugged
and waved him off, it had nothing to do with her.

The V-neck stared over at Jules for a long time from
the edge of the dance floor. Finally, he gave up and went
back to his table in defeat. His date looked very, very
bored. Jules watched the young man tell a funny story
to recapture the mood. The rower looked over at Jules
once more, who stared back at him, enjoying his fear,
his shaky, virginal voice, his nerves out of control.
Finally, the college boy turned his chair to face the wall,
away from Jules.

To his surprise, Jules felt a little ashamed of himself. His
mood was changing, his special night's charge was dying
down but he wanted to keep the feeling going, to do

something special with it—instead he'd ended up in another bar watching TV. He motioned to the waitress to bring him another quart, and when she brought it he surprised himself again. He had over three hundred dollars in his pocket for the starter motor. Normally in the city he'd hold it under the table and pull out one bill to pay, but this time he held all the bills out in front of his face. He took a long time pulling out the right bill, counting the money first in plain view. He wasn't even aware of what he was doing until he saw the waitress' eyes.

The young man and his date were gone. The lights faded and the music slowed from high to low, La Bamba to Old Man River, and then back to normal.

At the next table a group of young women sat laughing, they looked good, thought Jules as he got up to go to the washroom, smart and having fun in their black clothes and pink and green hair. But as he stood in the smoky gloom he almost stepped full onto one of their feet—trying to avoid it he staggered, putting his hand out to catch himself and grabbing at the edge of their table for balance. Instead he pulled the table cloth and their drinks fell, one straight into a young woman's lap, she yelled in alarm at her suddenly soaked black dress, half-standing and her face turning to fury. People looked and smiled with delight and someone clapped once. To his amazement Jules felt drunk, like he hadn't felt in years. He tried to pull himself together and get away from her angry eyes and her swearing mouth, knocking his way through the standing and dancing crowd and escaping to the back of the room.

The washrooms were full, he knew they were for drug use more than anything and he leaned against the back window to wait. He was fine. His heart was  slowing. As he watched the pool game he realized the owner's nephew was standing close beside him, he looked like his uncle in the photo but out of shape and with a lot less luck. Jules turned away from him toward the window, staring into black space. The nephew moved closer, an inch away, put his hand on Jules' shoulder and whispered in his ear, *Go home.* Jules could smell the nephew's breath and could guess his pudgy, ugly expression. He tried to push off the hand, but it didn't move, he recognized it was a strong, working hand. The voice whispered in his ear again, *I'm telling you twice now... go home! Hey, you hear me? Get lost. Beat it, man... this is your last chance.* Jules slowly turned to look at the man who was six inches shorter than him and about the same weight. He saw that the nephew was staring right through him to somewhere else, like a good machine just doing its job. Jules saw too that both the nephew and the young rower belonged there more than he did. He turned away again to the window, mumbling into his chest, *Fuck yourself.*

Suddenly the back of Jules' coat was over his head, he was bent double, blind, and before he could react pulled along by his tangled arms through the yelling room, glasses smashed and a corner of the oak bar came crashing sideways into his ribs, Jules yanked his arms down and down again to get them free, but he was tied like a headless farm animal still being towed at high speed across the dance floor with glimpses of the bouncer's thick legs and work boots calmly walking backwards, for fun knocking Jules sideways into the old juke box before finally swinging him wide like a baseball bat and letting go. Still blind Jules crashed backwards through the doorway and out into the narrow stairwell, landing in a pile of arms and legs on the upper landing—he instinctively covered his face curling into a ball as the nephew came out raising a big boot, but it stopped in mid-air when the owner yelled something from inside.

Jules felt a hand grabbing the back of his collar, picking him up like he weighed nothing, uncurling him and facing him down the steep stairwell—again, he instinctively twisted his body at the last minute and was thrown crashing into a wall—he fell backwards into space, reaching wildly, his hand grabbing the handrail for a second, just in time and turning in the air he somehow caught himself for a few steps, tripping on his own legs and free-falling down the last stairs—putting out his arms in time to save his head and crashing hard on his shoulder, rolling and landing flat on his back on the concrete sidewalk.

People were getting into a big, shiny car beside him, they stopped to look. They were dressed-up for a special night out, thought Jules, maybe a celebration dinner, or just to look fine. He became aware of himself through the expressions on their faces: one disgust, two fear and one indifference at him lying in a curled lump at their

feet, his scraped hands and bleeding face. They got into the car and
he heard the power doors lock.

HARD-LIMPING AND SORE he finally found his car again, he
got in carefully and sat still for a long time in the quiet,
the familiar wheel and gauges like a black jet cockpit, his
beautiful old car. He started the engine, revved it once
like an old lion making sure it could still roar and drove
into the downtown, into the start of another downpour.
He loved the car, it was like an extension of his own
body, he changed lanes instantly, winding through the
slow traffic, accelerating where there was space and
decelerating, changing gears, the flash of the car's black
and gold body and the rumble of the engine turning
heads, a rocking song blasting on the radio and outside
the windshield it was all electric, life, it was good.

He came onto a side street, looking for more space to
open up the car, gaining speed through the sleeping
neighbourhood, faster and finally punching into top
gear, the rear tires breaking loose for a second as his
lights fell onto a blurred object in the rain ahead, he
wasn't sure. It was a skinny teenaged girl standing in the
middle of the street, her group of friends had jumped to
the curb yelling but she was frozen, wide-eyed but calm,
waiting while the beautiful black car bore down on her

from nowhere. Jules knew there was no time to stop on the slick road. Without slowing he flicked the steering wheel, the car darted to one side at the last minute, there might be enough room to squeeze between her and the parked cars and he threaded the needle between them, howling by an inch from her thin body.

Several blocks away, he slowed to a snail's pace in first gear. He turned up the radio to full volume but it jarred him, his head hurt so he turned it off. The road he was on was deserted, lined by old, three storey buildings with spiraling staircases just visible in the pounding rain, approaching an ARRET sign he came to a halt and waited there. There was no cross traffic. The engine mumbled low and steady, it didn't have a brain, it was all muscle, strong and thick like a schoolyard bully. Rain bounced high off the big bird painted on the hood.

He drove slowly out turning onto the next street and barely pressing the accelerator while his mind replayed the experience: the lit figure of the girl—the car had performed well and so had his nerves—her calm face, her really not caring—halfway through the turn his foot pressed the gas, the engine screamed as the rear wheels broke loose and spun wildly on the wet road with the car fish-tailing to one side. His foot stayed stamped down hard like it had a will of its own while he adjusted in the direction of the skid, the car corrected bringing its rear end back into line but it kept going and fish-tailed to the other side the rear wheels still spinning at high speed. Jules corrected again, enjoying the response to the slight movements of his wrist. But without warning, the tires suddenly caught traction on the wet asphalt. The Firebird shot forward, jumped the curb and buried its front end into the trunk of a large maple.

He watched in slow motion as the bird on the hood folded like an accordion. The windshield went white and disappeared. It was dark.

Stopped, he realized he was stopped and he could only see through one eye, he put his hand to his face and it was red when he took it away. He wanted to get out of the city and he turned the key uselessly in the ignition, all he could hear was the familiar, *click, click* (*Reste tranquille, there's no panic.*) He sat, not wanting to leave the car. Finally he shoved hard and the door fell open with a loud metal creak and groan, one leg hurt a lot but he could still walk.

At the open trunk he reached in for the broom handle but it slipped out of his fingers, clattering back inside. He looked at his red hand like it wasn't his any more. He felt the familiar dull, throbbing ache. As he reached in again he stopped, seeing the exposed corner of the near-empty box of explosives under an old blanket. The dark, exciting emotions he'd brought to town were gone and the thick pane of glass was back between himself and the rest of the world. He wrapped the box in the blanket and hiked it onto his back.

The alarm in his head rang louder and louder. At the end of the block there was a power relay station, with a fence around it and a sign every few feet: a man dancing in a lightning bolt, his arms and legs flying.

3
Blue Black

58

... She didn't know why she hid under the blankets—she heard him re-enter the room and suddenly his lion head, brown hoary curls ranged on her neck and his teeth on her nipple—licking, his tongue the wing of a dark bird, the whole sky, the red dark orange fire light through the seams, her talons bleeding his pale back, baby's skin— he pulled out of the blankets, exposing her legs and her wetness to the room's cool air but from the waist up she stayed inside and his scaly hands pulled her thighs apart, he put his finger in and his wing again, rising and falling on her—she rose up higher and higher to meet him, his arms and legs climbing inside her into her dark aerie, her rain-soaked nest, she was in her horror sky—she heard, she might be laughing—his rude beard on her thighs, hands carrying her over and over, his black broad feathered back, winging her, winging her.

There was a purple stain

on the back of her Dad's head and neck where no hair would grow, he'd rub it absent-mindedly while he watched TV. One day she asked him where it came from, it was his first year as a volunteer fireman, a burning shed exploded, there were barrels of chemicals inside. He said he was partly turned away and a big, invisible fist knocked him flat to the ground. His two best friends were killed. Standing beside him. A look flashed in his eyes for an instant as he spoke it, at that moment Wendy could see the flames, and his fear—she couldn't help feeling glad, to see something there at all.

Wendy grew up in a remote logging-tourist town on Vancouver Island, the big debate the year she left was whether to install the first street lamps, Dad said it was hard to sleep with all that light coming in the windows. The day she turned sixteen, he told her she had a *real* mother and father, that her birth mother was half-Native, a *half-breed* he said and her birth father was white, but they weren't sure, it was just a good guess. Mommy had been her blood enemy for years but this made it official. They'd both tried so many times, the strain growing until it would all crack open again, they'd be screaming at each other again. And Dad staring at the Zenith.

She finally knew where her eyes came from.

WHEN IT WAS TIME TO GO AWAY to university, she made it almost to another country, Montreal. The night before catching the bus south to the Vancouver ferry she dyed her hair black, *Blue-Black*, it said on the box. But in Montreal it turned out to be in fashion so she still looked very white. Downtown she'd walk by the rare Native person, she couldn't remember not being afraid of them. She wondered if they could tell.

Wendy studied hard and went out with lots of boys, after a while their faces becoming a blur. The sex was almost always bad, she thought it was her fault. The girls she met all bragged about the size of their orgasms so she did too. She wondered what colour skin and eyes a baby of hers would have.

WENDY HAD SURVIVED her first city winter, it was the first warm day in April and she wore all black with her flowing vinyl-black hair, dark rouged lips and a long, velvet cape she'd made herself. She ran alone twirling in the Parc Jeanne-Mance, the air sweet and pungent and the bared earth steaming, buds breaking out of limbs and the playing fields shining wet—the sudden Quebec spring reached inside and stirred her, the sun on her hungry skin and her cape flowing out in circles as she spun on the luminous green. She had strong black wings and in those days she really thought she could fly.

Mommy died of throat cancer during April exams. It was sudden and Wendy didn't get out in time, she decided to stay away, she imagined Dad sitting, watching hockey or his *Dallas* reruns.

She got a job for the summer as a cashier-waitress in Old Montreal.

SHE'D JUST GOTTEN HER FIRST CONTRACT at the station when she met Jules. It was at a Christmas party in an Old Ville loft where she hardly knew anyone. It turned out Jules had been walking around the narrow, cobblestone streets, he'd followed the noise and just come in. No one stopped him. That was typical Jules.

Her date was awful, he was a young film producer, all he could talk about was how much things cost, he must have said the word *million* every second sentence. It was in the kitchen. Jules almost mowed her down coming in and he sat alone at the table, he looked at her a couple of times and she noticed his head turn when she went to the bathroom. He knew enough to give her time to look at him too, and he was worth looking at. She remembered him from years before at the restaurant when she noticed the mill scars on his ridiculously big hands. There was a bottle of tequila and a bottle of 7-UP on the counter and without thinking she turned to him and asked if he knew how to make *tequila bombs*, she was desperate for relief from the Million Dollar Man. Jules said no, but she sat with him anyway and made them herself, one for her and one for Jules and another for her date who decided to join them at the table, looking very pissed-off. Jules knew what to do. She showed him how and as they banged their glasses on the table and shot back their exploding drinks, over and over, it proved that Wendy and Jules could hold their liquor well—and Wendy's date became more and more drunk, the movie budgets getting bigger as his voice slurred.

Finally the tequila ran out and they sat for a while in respectful silence looking at the empty white bottle. Wendy's date got up awkwardly, found a bottle of vodka and announced he was going to make *vodka bombs*. He poured a full three inches of liquor into two glasses, added just a dash of pop and passed one to Jules. He banged his own glass down hard on the retro Formica, almost breaking the glass and mumbling something about *real men*, and he drank it all down, suddenly bending over double, coughing and gasping for several minutes. When he finished, he turned to Jules and said, very drunkenly, *Hey, aren't you gonna drink yours?*

Jules looked at him, as if he'd only just seen him, and said, *Is that for me? No, I never mix drinks.* He said it with a straight face, and they watched as Wendy's date suddenly staggered off in a hurry to the washroom.

Wendy was alone in the kitchen with Jules. Initially she'd had just a little interest in him, he was a bit young, around her own age she guessed. But what she liked most  was that he didn't talk much, it was refreshing. She leaned closer to him, *Jesus, what a charmer*, she whispered, raising her eyebrows comically in the direction of the washroom down the hall where they could hear her date throwing up. At that moment there was a tiny spark in Jules' eyes, a glint of humour and intelligence— the way he looked right inside her. She asked him what he did for a living. She thought he looked angry for a second, but he said simply, *I work in a plywood mill.* She didn't mind. After all, the mill workers were the well-paid heroes where she came from. He said she'd changed her hair. She'd dyed it back almost to her native auburn when she graduated from university. He didn't say much after that, Wendy did the talking, she even shushed him a couple of times and he sat, obedient, like he could hear her thinking, *Don't talk, don't say a word. Don't spoil it.*

They left the party and played in the snow, laughing and drunk at 20° below. They threw snowballs at each other all the way to her new home in a condo tower beside the student ghetto. In front of her building Jules reached for her. He held her ribs a little too tightly for their first kiss, like he couldn't believe what he held, and the slow, wide river that had begun flowing inside her at the party suddenly became a roaring current.

They made love without saying a word the whole night except for one—every time he tried to come inside, or even touch her there, she'd say, *No.* Until finally, to her amazement, she heard sweet, dancing laughter that must have been hers. He seemed awkward and unsure, so she finally helped him inside, wrapping her legs around him. Then she noticed his face. He was in such pain.

THE LAST TIME WENDY DRANK it was with Jules. It was the last straw. They were both still trying to find the formula that had brought them together that first night—and one of the ingredients was alcohol, they were afraid of each other without it. That night they went to a rock concert. They drank before, in the lobby bar during the concert, and all night after. But neither of them could get drunk any more, not at all, they were that soaked in it.

She realized later that they drank for opposite reasons, that Jules drank to get in touch with his emotions and she drank so she wouldn't feel so damned much. So when they drank together they were going in opposite directions and there was just a small space to meet in, where they both felt a similar amount. During their weeks together they kept trying to meet in that tiny little space. But they'd keep on drinking and he'd be feeling more and she'd be feeling less and less—back where they started but on opposite sides.

It was at the concert that he told her what he considered his darkest secret, the thing he felt the most guilty about. He said he was sure he had a child, somewhere, out there. He thought it was a son. He didn't know where, or who the mother was, but he said he could *feel* him out there. He said he woke up nights with the certainty that his child needed him at that moment. But he'd slept with so many different women he didn't know where to start looking.

Wendy told him it was just his paternal instinct, his imagination, that all men wanted a son. She was furious, he was trying to talk himself into feeling something. But for her, his story seemed pathetic. And it was something more she'd have to forget. So she told him something to try and feel, she told him about her two abortions, describing them in graphic detail. She told him about the last one, the doctor was very rough with her, he was angry, he said he didn't want to do it because it was her second, but he had to because it was his job. After that, in the following weeks she became very ill. Finally, she went back into hospital and they found half the foetus still inside of her. He'd left it there. To teach her a lesson.

That night they didn't say much more, just drank and drank in silence.

The next day he was gone.

WENDY HAD SLEPT through the entire day. When she got up it was almost 8:00 pm, July the 1st, Canada Day! She'd been working later and later as the summer increased, after broadcast with everyone gone home she'd stay to research an interview, and other things she could schedule for the daytime but increasingly didn't. Sometimes she arrived home as the first shades of bruise-blue showed in the sky, she'd finally go to bed after watching the sunrise and sleep right through until evening.

Outside her fourteenth storey window a burnt-orange sun lit the tallest towers in the business core and the wider, east-west corridors. She watched the smaller streets below turning a smudged blue-black, one by one. Holiday traffic was headed for the riverfront, for the federal government's massive fireworks display. She turned on the television. She turned it off, then on again. She turned it back off, then on and off several more times. Finally she inserted a video into the VCR, it was a tape of herself interviewing a science media celebrity. The man's hands waved in the air as he spoke in a friendly, cheerful tone as if speaking to children, *Scientists have actually managed to graft a small plant with a firefly, so that now the plant glows in the dark! Who knows the potential of such a discovery? Perhaps in the future we will no longer need electricity for light.*

On-screen she leaned forward to display her interest, *Are you saying, Doctor, that one day we could have glowing house plants instead of lamps in our homes?*

Who knows, and trees instead of street-lights, whole parks and forests we could stroll through after dark. The ramifications could be enormous... What is it you women say? Perhaps we could finally 'Bring back the night?'

That's 'take back the night'.

Maybe this is possible.

Wendy looked a little skeptical, *With science?*

Her index finger pressed the STOP button and she headed for the door.

IN THE GARAGE UNDER HER BUILDING Wendy rounded a concrete pillar and came suddenly face to face with the Security Guard and his psychotic doberman, whenever she saw him with that dog she remembered an item she'd read: *Years of breeding for aggressiveness have caused the front of their skulls to press in on the brain—they spend their lives in near-constant mental anguish.* The dog made an aborted leap at her, choking and straining at the end of its chain, its growling and explosive bark bouncing off the cement walls, but the athletic-looking guard yanked hard on the chain as she skirted around them towards her car, wondering if the dog wanted to bite or lick her. As its jaws opened and closed inches from her waist the overhead lights began to flicker. She looked up as they went out.

Crisse-tabernac! said the guard in the pitch dark turning on his flashlight and shining it straight into Wendy's eyes. She waved her hand in front of her face and he moved the beam away. Peering into the gloom Wendy worked hard to suppress her panic. *Looks like someone pulled the plug,* she shrugged. *Will you help me find my car please?*

The electric doors won't open without power, Ms. Holiday.

Well then, I guess I'll have to take a cab.

In the darkened lobby the guard shone his flashlight so she could tie a scarf over her head in the mirror, trying to hide her hair as best she could, *What am I doing anyway? No one will be able to see me tonight.* She stuffed the scarf into her purse as a taxi pulled up and sounded its horn.

Riding through the darkened streets the city was barely recognizable without power, the familiar route she drove each night was without its usual landmarks, no theatre marquees, dépanneur beer and cigarette signs or traffic lights changing red-green-yellow-red. Only the occasional bar or cafe glowed dimly with flickering candlelight. In the taxi's headlights and those of other cars she caught glimpses of a few people out strolling, despite the dark, she guessed it was the heat with their air conditioners out of order. The nearly coal-black-skinned driver looked at Wendy in the mirror whenever another car lit the cab's interior, he turned halfway round towards her, his elbow on the back of the seat and he spoke with a deep-voiced, sugar-cane Jamaican accent, *You're Wendy Holiday, aren't you, from the*

Late News. I watch you every night. She
smiled half-heartedly, not wanting
to encourage him so he'd turn
back to face the road, *Yes, that's me.*

They drove on in silence until
the driver turned back again, she wished he'd face
forward, if only to drive down the blackened street. He
spoke slowly and calmly, she was surprised, despite
herself, at how educated he sounded. And his voice was
somehow calming. *Excuse me for asking, I've been wanting to
know. When my neighbour, young Marvin Louis was shot by the
Police last month for nothing, why'd you stick a camera in his
mother's crying face and make her angry, so she ended up yelling on
the TV? Her boy's dead, why couldn't you leave her alone?*

She shrunk down in her seat, remembering the clip
and knowing exactly what he meant, *I don't make those
decisions. I'm sorry if, I guess it is intrusive. It's true. I don't like our
remotes at times like that.*

*I understand. It's not you who makes the news. You just read it.
You're just doing your job, hmm?* At that moment the car's
engine started to sputter. It stalled and the driver sighed
heavily and pushed the lever to N, coasting and turning
the key uselessly. He pulled the taxi over to the curb.
Damn it, he whispered angrily, putting the meter on
hold. *I'm sorry, please forgive this inconvenience.* He stepped
out of the car and raised the hood.

Wendy rolled down the window and stared ahead into
the gloom. After a few cars passed, she was sure the
building where she worked was just around the corner.
On an impulse she got out of the cab and held out a bill

to pay off the driver. He was bent over fiddling with levers and hoses and looked up at her in surprise, *I've almost got it fixed lady. Please, go sit in the cab.*

She pushed the bill, which was much larger than the fare, into the driver's hand. *Thank you very much for the ride,* she said, turning and walking quickly away. Behind her the driver's voice was plaintive and a little annoyed, *Lady, please wait. It's not safe.*

At the next corner she paused, trying consciously to adjust her eyes to the darkness. A car passed and she could see for a second down the once-familiar street. Then it was full dark again. She started off, fighting back her fear. It was as if she could see it in her mind, her stuffing it back into its room and slamming the door, like she'd always done. The night was a huge black hand squeezing her. She put distance between herself and the cab. Was it her imagination that the darkness had a blue tinge like they used in movies to pretend it was night? It occurred to her that without lights it was no more dangerous than usual. It might even be safer. No one could see her. It was like night-time in the country when she was little, there was a privacy she wasn't used to any more.

But the sounds were different: an unseen window smashing, a car alarm playing six quick, sharp tunes over and over, a snatch of laughter suddenly stopped, someone's cough, sirens echoing in a far-off neighbourhood. Wendy began to doubt which street she was on after all. Then her heart jumped. Someone was walking close behind. She froze where she stood, she couldn't move a muscle, she felt silly, and furious, like a stupid jack rabbit huddled on the highway waiting to be run over. Whoever it was had also stopped in the dark. She  listened hard, straining, holding her breath so she could hear and waiting for a break in the night sounds, but her heart was beating so loudly in her ears. She wasn't sure, but she thought she could hear someone breathing.

Suddenly feet broke into a run in the darkness nearby, many feet. A car turned the corner ahead and from out of the darkness a group of small children appeared running past her on both sides, brushing her legs and shifting her dress. In the car's highbeams their little bodies took shape then vanished down the throat of an alley and were gone.

The car was past and Wendy shook her head in disbe-lief. She had just started on her way again when she stumbled on something soft. She stepped back quickly, blind and afraid, and felt ahead tentatively with her foot, before seeing in another far-off headlight that the soft object was the curled, pathetic figure of a man. He looked up at her through the crook of his arm. *I'm, I'm sorry*, she said as she took a wary step back, *Are you ... all right?*

He mumbled through his arm, *Ya ... I'm fine.* Wendy shivered, suddenly shaken to her core. An ice-cold current ran through her bones and for a moment she was unsure of what to do. Finally she shrugged ner-vously, stepped around him with a wide berth and walked quickly away, tossing her head as if to shake the fear from it.

At the next corner she could just make out the tall, black outline of the Broadcast Corporation building where she worked. It had been right overhead but its dark stone facade was blended in with the sky, in the surrounding poor neighbourhood they called it the *black tower* and tonight it really was.

Then the lights came back on and everything was back to normal, Wendy ran towards the building's entrance.

WENDY SAT ON A STOOL in the Bar-Taverne Américaine not far from the station with Marie-Anne, the producer of the Late News. Marie-Anne, as usual, spoke with her hand waving in circles and a voice revealing years of cigarettes and sarcasm. The Américaine was filled with wagon wheels, stars and stripes, photos of big-busted movie stars and President Kennedy, red and black upholstery and dim pink and blue lighting. A few customers huddled in the shadows as a woman in her late sixties entered quietly from the street and stepped up carefully to the small stage, three long haired musicians backed her, two in biker leathers and the third wearing a jacket sewn from an American flag, the old singer spoke in a wispy voice like a small bird's, *This*

is a song I learnt in Rio deee Janeiro. She
held her hands out in front of her,
pressing the insides of her wrists
together with her fingers curling in
at the top to form a heart shape.
Her hands framed a couple intently making out at a
table, a middle-aged Elvis and Marilyn Monroe. *This one's
for you two. Having a good cruise? How about the rest of you?
Mmmmm, I just love a man in a tux. Come on girls, take your pick.*
She began to sing The Girl From Ipanema, the first
verses in badly pronounced Portuguese. No one listened.

Wendy fingered her orange juice, *You know, when I was
younger I could always hear a kind of a voice inside, that I trusted.
It used to tell me what to do and when to do it.*

Marie-Anne nodded knowingly, *And who to do it with*,
she said.

Wendy motioned to the bartender for another juice
and steered the subject in another direction. She tried to
start a discussion of the night's lead story, but she knew
what was coming. Malcolm, her co-anchor, had been in
Marie-Anne's office when she arrived at work. She knew
from Marie-Anne's expression that it was time to stay
quiet and let her say her piece. *Wendy, he's really upset this
time. He says you're making it harder and harder for him, that he
never knows what to expect. He's right that you've gotta cut down
on the ad-libs. He has to follow a plan, he's that kind of guy. And
the jokes all the time. What's with you anyway...? This year, I
mean, you still do a good job, the ratings are O.K. but you don't
seem... happy... and you're always on your own now. What's eating*

you...? Marie-Anne paused, a series of irritated creases appearing on her forehead. *It's not your love life is it?*

Wendy laughed before checking herself, *No, hardly. I've decided to take a break from that. I'm fed up with the whole thing. I haven't even had a date in months.* Since Jules, she thought, before pushing him back where he belonged. *But I haven't given up hope for the long run, part of me still believes, after all this time, that I'll find my ideal lover.... You'd think I'd have given up by now.*

Marie-Anne studied her, looking a little disgusted. Wendy felt disappointed at Marie-Anne's attempt at sensitivity. She'd wanted some tough medicine. She'd wanted to get off the maudlin track she'd been down for months. Marie-Anne shifted uncomfortably on her stool, turned away and spoke quietly as if to the room itself, *Well, most men make dismal lovers.*

Wendy tried to hide her surprise. *Do you think women are any better?*

Not exactly, she still spoke to the room, looking irritated, at herself more than anyone, *Years ago I came to the conclusion, after much trial and much error, that women do make better lovers... But for other women.* She waited for Wendy's reaction to the station's biggest open secret. *And men for other men too. They have the same kinds of ... bodies.*

Marie-Anne was almost totally focused on her work. Wendy knew how rare this conversation was. *You mean a woman knows what it feels like, inside, to be a woman?* she said, suddenly feeling Jules' wrecked hands and thinking that sex wasn't their main problem. *I've thought about that, but I've just never felt much sexual attraction for women. I've tried to be honest with myself about it, because it would make for a wider search. But as far back as I can remember, it's always been men for me.*

Marie-Anne looked at her with genuine sympathy, *Well then, it probably always will be.* She lit a cigarette and changed the subject, relieved to move on. *You don't drink anymore, how come?*

Wendy cringed. She looked at her empty glass for a long moment, *You really want to hear it?*

I really want to hear it....

The old singer had finished her set. She stepped gingerly across the room and perched on the stool beside Wendy, giving her a knowing look. The band continued on-stage, the guitar and bass players facing their amps playing the Stars and Stripes with a slow and heavy beat and plenty of distortion.

MARIE-ANNE SPOKE THROUGH THE INTERCOM, *Mikes are off.* Malcolm was upset but trying not to show it, on the monitors the credits rolled over he and Wendy as they appeared to chat amiably.

Wendy, I wish you wouldn't do that, it really bothers me Wendy. Her lips moved in response but no sound came out, on screen she looked cheerful, she even touched him on the arm and broke into silent laughter. She knew how much it unnerved him but she couldn't stop, it was a compulsion.

Please, Wendy. That makes me really very uncomfortable.... The ON-AIR sign went out and Wendy was surprised herself at the way she jumped out of her chair, a camera had been left on beside a monitor, she pointed it at herself and quickly checked how she looked. Her makeup was still on but she decided it would be good to get out early for a change, she just wanted to be out of the building, outside.

She was downstairs in a minute but stopped in the dimly-lit lobby. She didn't know where to go, but she had to get out of there. She'd take a taxi straight home.

IN HER OWN BUILDING as the elevator doors opened the lights suddenly went out once more. *Just like that,* she said quietly, standing stock still and waiting for her eyes to adjust. She was surprised that no sound accompanied the moment the power stopped, no *click,* or *beep,* just suddenly an eerie nothing.

She decided to use the stairs, she wanted to get out of the lobby before the security guard and that damn dog showed up. It turned out the stairwell was dimly lit from the red SORTIE signs which must have been battery-powered. She pushed herself, the first few flights were easy enough but she began to tire, her breath was unusually tight, but she stepped up her pace even more, trying to get it over with and to the safety of her own home. She was becoming drenched in sweat, surprised how  quickly the building became stifling. She kept count of the floors and stopped to rest only when she reached the tenth, gasping for air and feeling sick in her stomach. She heard a door close several floors below and she started to run as best she could, when she finally staggered through the fire door on her own floor she was ready to collapse. She fumbled her key into the dark lock, stepped in and quickly shut the door behind her, sliding down the wall to sit on the floor, but the air was stifling in there too, she could barely breath and she groped her way across the black apartment, knocking into the furniture, bruising her shins and finally sliding open the balcony door, out into the fullness of the night air.

Stretching below her the city had become a few pretty white lines of cars, looming shadows that were once buildings and bottomless wells of pitch blackness. But her attention was taken, by a slight, cooler breeze blowing down lightly from the north, all her muscles, her body and soul sang to the tune and smell of this sweet air as she stretched in relief—she felt reckless with the multi-storey drop beneath her—the smell of the wind from the wild was filling her with new energy, taking her to places in the past when she felt free, not like an animal pacing in a cage. Leaning on the metal railing she pulled up on it hard, she half expected it to come off in her hands with the power she felt. Suddenly the lights came back on and Montreal appeared full before her eyes. But that smell had her physically connected to a thousand different memories. She decided.

In her bathroom she washed off the pancake and took out a theatrical makeup kit from her acting days in university. She practiced the walk in the mirror, and then without looking, she tried her best to *feel* it: hips still, willing her center of gravity upwards into her chest behind her strapped-down breasts. This alone made her feel taller, more confident—it was amazing, she felt a strange desire to lead people but she didn't know where to, it didn't matter. Did they all feel that? Some men's hips moved, but it wasn't the same as a woman's. It was smaller, with the pants slung low and the shoulders leading like a jungle cat. It was sexy, but most of them seemed to keep everything as still as possible below the neck. The young, butch woman at the video store, she walked like that, a caricature of a fifty-year-old man with a pound of undigested steak in his belly. She'd need to do better than caricature. Her life might depend on it.

The last thing was to pin down her hair and stuff it into her Greek fisherman's hat. The moustache was on straight. She was ready to go. She was finally going to do it.

SHERBROOKE STREET WAS STILL crowded with people, the downtown didn't really start until after midnight. As Wendy stepped out of the building's side exit she was  instantly sweating again in the wet heat, the jacket was like a portable sauna, a waft of stinging male body odour reached up from the arm pits, she'd bought it used on purpose partly for that smell and she'd added shoulder pads, it did the job. She wondered who it had come from, what he'd been like. The oversized shoes worked all right, the toes and heels were padded too. But she had to remember to keep her hands in her pockets, they were a dead giveaway. She had to concentrate.

Reaching the heart of downtown Wendy stood over a Metro vent as a train roared by under her, the stale draft drifting to her face. There was a mild hysteria in the crowd, fueled by the temperature but held in check by people's desire to move slowly and avoid sweating. There seemed to be hundreds of young men in cars driving slowly by, bass speakers shaking the ground. They didn't even look at her. Her heart galloped for an instant as a voice from a doorway hissed at her but she realized it was just a hash seller. People stepped around her without a glance. She felt invisible, it was magic, she could watch them at her leisure, since she was a little girl she couldn't remember feeling so anonymous, a spectator with the freedom to watch without being watched. She stopped, catching a reflection in a store window, a blurred silhouette of a slender young man standing against a bank of flashing neon on St. Catherine Street. He had a sensitive face, but he looked tough too. She liked him, but she wouldn't mess with him. It was like he was on a movie screen but she could control his movements, a leg, a shoulder.

It started to rain softly while she walked. Then it built quickly into a full downpour. She didn't mind, she liked it, until she remembered the makeup and touched her hand to her fake five o'clock shadow, stepping under the eve of a building. There were several banks of stacked TVs in the store window, all showing an ad for the Late News, a woman with an animated face repeated twelve times, her incandescent hair looked soft, like a baby's— her expression changed constantly, from deadly serious, to friendly, even sexy for a moment.

Wendy saw too, on the window pane in front of the sets, Jules' reflection looming behind her like the black hole that he was. His shadow rose up and over her head and merged with the night sky as an explosion wiped her face off the screens—and a huge, invisible fist flew through the air and knocked her off her feet.

Dangerous,
Unreliable
& Rude

FURY IN A HOUSE IN NEW WESTMINSTER,
JUNE 28, 1999 AT 7:10 AM:

... Summer death rain drilling into blacktop—cold bones death cold—life's remains turned under into earth—sleeping seed buried in me and your fields of golden laughter—I miss you.

Jacky didn't remember much

from his years in Vancouver, he was either on a binge or
drying out from one. Almost thirty years in Canada and
he'd worked the dockyards, the prairie harvest, on road
crews and construction labour, he'd driven dump trucks,
highway bus and nine years with Vancouver Transit
until he finally got fired from there too. He drove taxi
after that, he even tried being a gardener. He was still
good at getting jobs but not at keeping them. He could
always talk his way in, people liked and trusted him, he
never knew why. It was always a surprise. Eventually
he'd make them fire him if they were stubborn about it.

He never would have gotten on with Transit if the guy
hadn't taken such a shine to him. He told Jacky they'd
gotten a bad recommendation from Coachways, but he
did a good test drive and they were looking for a *certain
personality*, whatever that was. They could have fired him
a half dozen times over the years before they finally did,
he'd screwed up big but they always ignored it. Finally,
when he did get the boot it wasn't his fault. One day he
went into McDonald's to use the washroom and when
he came out the bus wasn't there. He thought it was
stolen, but it turned out to be a half block down the hill,
its front bumper pressed into a power pole. Luckily no
one was hurt but when the inspector arrived he canned

Jacky on the spot, right there on the street. They said it was officially *impossible* for the parking brake to come off on its own, that he hadn't set it before he got out. It was weird coming out of the McDonald's with a hot coffee, standing there and no bus, he even checked to see if he was in uniform. He could have fought it but he was secretly glad. He'd had a recurring nightmare for a year of him pounding the blunt front end of a bus with his bare fists.

He'd always wanted to just stop, to see what would happen, and in what order. There'd been a lot of sitting around lately. He was trying to remember who the Hell he was. The phone was disconnected, he'd recently sold the power tools to the Pakistani kid next door who made a crack to his friend about how they hadn't been used in a long time. One dark, slow-moving, cold day in June when summer was just a bad joke a truck pulled into the driveway, but there wasn't much left worth taking. The short, muscular man with a curled moustache was in charge, he said to Jacky when they were done, *There... now you've got some room to think!* He felt sorry for saying it and left the black & white portable behind, sitting alone on the floor.

Jacky wouldn't go outside. He'd stocked up on canned food and smokes. One morning the power was finally disconnected, he was long out of clean clothes and he got out the bag with the old-fashioned Coachways uniform he'd never returned. It smelled of rank mold and he put it on with the peaked hat too and looked in the long hallway mirror. In the dim bronze light from the frosted glass beside the door he saw his silhouette and got cold-sick in his stomach, for a second he thought it was his Da standing there. He'd been in the Dublin  Constabulary. Jacky'd never made the connection.

His Da talked Jacky out of becoming a policeman, he told him about putting down a food riot. He was ashamed of his job, but it was the only one he could find, he made sure Jacky did his homework and he passed on his love of reading.

Jacky heard a noise in the lock, it was Jesse the land-lord trying to find the right key. Jacky put on the long raincoat he used to wear to hide the Transit uniform so he could go straight to the bar, and when he unlocked the door Jesse physically pulled him out and shut the door behind him. Jacky didn't even look back, just got in his faded Plymouth Fury and drove away.

JACKY HAD A LETTER folded in his pocket. Six months before he'd hired an agency, they had an ad in a flyer saying they traced people. The letter said Gloria had disappeared *without a trace* back in '79. But she had a daughter, born in Calgary General Hospital, adopted out.... A possible present address was included in Montreal, she had red hair.

Jacky bought three mickeys of Metaxa brandy at the government liquor store and a giant-sized Mohawk Gas dashboard cup of coffee. He pointed the car onto the bridge east and stepped on it, his back to the rain-soaked city.

He drove straight all the way across, not sleeping for four days and nights, just pulling over now and then to rest in his seat. He'd discovered years before that he couldn't sleep unless he was horizontal, no matter how tired he got. The second he was dropping off, he'd wake up again, over and over, sliding down into the dark but always waking up again. Even so, after Thunder Bay in the middle of the night he got out the old baggy of pills a trucker had sold him years before. *Speed*, he'd said they were, *Made 'specially for driving*.

LATE ON THE FOURTH NIGHT Jacky parked his Fury in the east end of downtown Montreal, the fuel gauge was on E and the last of the power tool money was gone. He was pretty screwed up—everything swam together like a moving painting there was so much to look at—and he badly needed to find a safe place to lie down, for a couple of days. He felt unsteady and put his hand on the roof of a parked car, standing with his legs wide like John Wayne with cancer at his last Academy Awards, he walked slowly down rue St. Catherine in the thick, humid heat, the uniform soaked through under the raincoat. A group of bald young women in black army fatigues strode by. Their bare arms slow swung like  pendulums as they passed a cluster of old ladies in mourning, over his head neon women were bent-over in tall, round M's with their breasts blinking and legs spread open in wide V's, it was the time of day photographers call *the magic hour*, the last sun raking the old buildings with hot light, strained faces becoming beautiful, the broken streetscape leaning back and stretching and hundreds of electric signs rising up out of the scene like brilliant fruit: *Bonjour Bon Prix Hot Women and Cold Beer! Sexe Non-Stop Sexe-Plus Sexo-theque Boutique de Sexe Frites-French Fries Videoxxx Strip Teaseuses Cinema-Eve Casanova's Animatrice Pour Couple Patates Peep Show Palais d'Amusement Midway Milliooooonnaire Loto le Cinema le Plus Hot en Ville! Le Meilleur Hot Dog Ultra Delicieuses Bonne Fete Canada—Happy Canada Day, Venez Goutez—Come and Taste!* And real-live women whispered and laughed from doorways as he passed. Behind iron bars in an appliance store window a young woman spoke to him from three banks of TV sets, she had long licks of flame-coloured hair against a teal blue background. *Why*, she asked him in a tone of warm authority, *Are individuals becoming obsessed with one celebrity, with tragic results including an assassination attempt on Ronald Reagan, former President of the United States, or the actual death of John Lennon? Why are these lonely individuals confusing imagined personal relationships with reality? Tune in tonight.* Her lips opened and closed, her rose petal skin that he wanted to touch.

Thunder rolled in the distance as he turned a corner onto on a side street where a wire mesh fence surrounded a power sub-station, a loud, angry hum like an alarm emanated from the gigantic gray metal boxes. A sign at face-level was posted every few feet: inside a red circle a man was being stuck-through by a lightning bolt. Jacky found himself walking down a deserted, narrow street past crumbling buildings and over-flowing garbage. The only dim light was from a single, weak streetlamp receding behind him. He stopped in his tracks as there was a hollow metal crash nearby, a snatch of stifled laughter and in the distance a man and woman yelled at each other from a high window. Shivering, he pulled his coat close around him. A voice came out of the shadows, *Hey, dipstick! Give us your money.*

He looked in the direction the voice came from, down, at a boy, about twelve years old. He sounded patient, almost bored, *Vas-y, C'mon, hand it over.* Jacky shrugged and shook his head. After a while he said, *I... don't have anything.* His voice was dried-out, he hadn't said a word to anyone in over three weeks. He tried to peer into the musty dark and realized the boy wasn't alone, that ten or fifteen more boys and girls were playing in the deep shadows. There was a long scraping sound on the pavement that he didn't recognize and Jacky was hit hard from behind by a skateboarder. He fell onto his knees and a high-pitched howl went up as the children moved in on him. Suddenly their hands were all over his body, some going through his raincoat pockets and others pulling him with their combined weight towards the ground, he held his coat closed at the  throat and waist with all his strength while they kicked and punched his legs and chest, pulling on his arms, his hair, a mini hand yanking down on the back of his collar—he saw flashes of their little, determined faces but it was mainly their grasping and tearing hands—the lone, distant streetlight swirled in and out of view while a little thumb dug into the front of his throat—finally, he couldn't resist their weight any longer—they pulled him crashing down onto his side—their voices whispered and distorted as they kicked him in the head, the throat and the groin.

They suddenly gave up and ran away, leaving him still gripping his coat closed. He didn't know why he didn't want them to see the uniform. It started to rain. He lay still in a foetal heap, drops leaping from the puddle by his face.

MAYBE IT WAS A DREAM. It was pitch dark, he could hear the city around him, but couldn't see a thing. Suddenly there she was, towering over him, a passing car lighting her from behind and making a shimmering halo around her, her hair glowed like a bonfire lit from inside. Then it was dark again. He heard her apologize and walk quickly away.

HE WOKE LATER to the sound of a nearby explosion, the darkness lighting up with fire and flames shooting through the air while the earth rocked like a jackhammer under his body—it lasted a few seconds the smashing of hundreds of windows and thudding debris falling all around him—it was quiet for a few seconds more, and then people yelling—sirens.

A moment later a young man in a leather jacket leaned over him, silhouetted against flashing red lights on the walls. He had a beautiful face, like an angel in a church, with a strand of long, red hair falling out of his hat and down his cheek. They both looked up as more explosions erupted in the night sky—the holiday fireworks had started. Wendy smelled a slip of cool, sweet air entering her, stirring her more awake than she'd ever been. Jacky lay staring up at the blurry colours and explosions. They reminded him of the northern lights.

Gloria.

□

PIERCE

Paradise,

our new neighbour Piers calls it. He says his name *Pierce*, like with an SS, he's from London, England. He means Vancouver's a paradise, where we've just moved. Piers changes how he looks all the time, but as if with shadows. I keep seeing him in the road outside and not recognizing him. One day he looks like a cool young European guy, handsome and relaxed, manly, with very short hair almost like a skinhead, the way he walks hips rolling easy and everything's a game or a joke over here, in *fucking Canada man*, which he says a lot, shaking his head at his own good fortune.

Other times he's wearing a yellow and black CAT hat, working on one of his 70's Japanese motorbikes. The kind that are a little fat and not so loud, *four strokes*, he says, not high and whiney like the newer *two strokes* with the low curving windshields that drive around and around the block late at night like a dentist drilling into your bone, or the old Harleys with their fixed mufflers to make that blasting sound and you can't hear a thing while they're going by. He complains it's all doctors and lawyers buying them up now, in their brand new leathers and little Shultz helmets with a day-and-a-half's growth on their puffy self-conscious middle class faces.

Born To Be Mild, my wife Mandy says on the back porch, and Piers laughs.

I've noticed the same phenomenon, and I say that for some reason the gay bikers seem O.K. maybe because they're not really imitating anyone, they've made up something new that's just for them. *Fuckin' leather boys*, he says.

Then his father shows up for a week from England, sleeping on a thrown-out mattress on their kitchen floor. He wears an ascot and his hair is carefully swept in silver waves, he speaks and acts like an English theatre actor. Piers is really excited about his Dad, he's smiling nice all week, but there's an almost visible knife-edge. He told us once about growing up mostly alone, and in jail during his teens.

Piers fixes up old motorbikes *to sell*. I think really he's collecting them in his basement, but he has to say he's selling them so Surinder, his wife, can't say he isn't trying to bring in money. She works in a Robson Street boutique, rides her ten speed off each morning and arrives home at dinner. Sometimes she looks sad under her dayglo-green helmet riding into the back lane. Other times she smiles and she looks like a different person too, but it's more like a normal person looks different. When Piers doesn't shave for a week with an old baseball hat and he's fixing a rusty roof rack onto his old Malibu, I think it's some guy down from Vanderhoof for the long weekend to see his smart little sister who went to UBC and bought a house worth half a million now, he bought his split-level in Vanderhoof last year *for* $31,000! and he's out there in the street trying to tighten the jammed bolt, looking around from under his hat at the rich people and listening to the birds chirp. His brother-in-law thinks he's dumb but he isn't, he just stayed in Vanderhoof.

So. Piers changes, but like today when a new shadow's fallen over his face and his clothes are a little different again, he smiles like a happy boy and I like him again, until I meet him in the driveway and he says, *Hey, it's Mr. Renovator*, like it's a dig, and I'm suddenly not as cool as him because I'm not from Europe and I bother painting my half of the house even though we're renting and I'm making the owner fix the hole in the kitchen ceiling and a lot of other small stuff. Stuff Piers might fix himself with a bit of wire or some glue and a block of wood. So I like him one second and I don't the next.

He tells me his friends have always been women, and I understand why, but I don't say it. The next time he makes a crack, it's that he heard us *complaining about money* the other night. Mandy mentions to him she's still looking for waitress work and he says it then, all smiles, planting it like a bad seed. I remember the fight a couple of nights before, with the window open behind the closed curtain and maybe he was standing two feet away on the sidewalk. Because he's always out there, working on the 50's lawn mower he brought home, someone else's garbage. I was lying on the couch and her standing hands on hips like she does, and she'd been on my case for not being *available* to her and for being a black cloud. I knew it too. I'm like death in the house when I'm under pressure. But she gets weird too, and when she does I leave her alone to figure it out. That's not her style though, she tries to dive right into whatever I'm feeling, and that night I'd been telling and telling her to just leave me alone and finally, I started yelling at her all the stuff that was freaking me out, like we'd spent a fortune moving and there wasn't a lot left and my work wasn't bringing in much yet, and we just might run out of dollars soon and there was a mountain on top of me. A-whole-fucking-mountainous-mountain. I told her all the work I had to do before I could fix it so we'd keep going forward and not back again, so I wouldn't have to go back to driving truck or cab and on and on. I felt really bad then and she felt just as bad, I'd convinced her then it was true, that I had this Mount Everest on top of me and to just leave me goddamn-it alone while I figured it out. And she went off to bed on her own. And I woke up in the middle of the night cruddy and curled-up like a baby on the green velvet couch we inherited from her ex-step-mother's Great Dane. We had the odour cleaned out.

Piers must have heard me *complaining about money*. And today, he's out there tying a red and silver 12 foot aluminum car-topper, that he bought *for only $15!* onto the roof rack of his car he bought *for $200!* to fix up and sell *fucking Canada man!* I can't help staring at the boat and I tell him it's the exact one my father bought at Sears when I was a little kid. He took me out in it for years, trolling back and forth in the gray rain.

And I think: *I grew up here and I did that Piers, and you didn't.* When I was older, in my teens, I was usually sleeping-off hangovers on weekends but my Dad still went out on his own at six am. When I was seventeen he finally sold the car-topper and bought a 24 foot cabin cruiser with a flying bridge, a kitchen and a stereo, to lure me out I think. I went out in it twice, but we both knew it wasn't right. The 12-foot was better, but it was gone and anyway you can't go back. My father was in a bad mood all the time then. Or maybe I'd started to mind it more. He didn't seem to like us. He was away most of the time on business trips and I was sort of the mini-Dad in his place.

Now I don't want to go out in boats.

I guess Piers can't get his life in gear. He talks with my wife on the back porch a lot lately, saying how it's great he and Surinder are still in love and saying, *Wow, he's motivated*, about me, as Mandy describes what I'm trying to do. But he says it like a dig too, like it's middle class and uncool to do anything except roam the grassy alleys at night looking for 'abandoned' bicycles to bring home, anything else is only to do with money or power. And I wonder if I'm just imagining it, but I know I'm not. I can tell the difference.

Piers spends his time fixing broken machines nobody wants. And I do like him sometimes. Yesterday, he told me his Dad died.

Soon I'm going to ask him to take me out in that boat, *used only once for four hours, twenty years ago*. I want us to troll into the middle of English Bay, out beside the resting freighters, waiting there like dark, hulking fathers.

JESUS

JESUS

JESUS

On my side

in the sleeper of a mammoth truck driven by a blonde boy with a stringy moustache—it was an Extra Wide Load with an amber light strobing off the cab's roof, the kind they only allowed on the road at night with a gargantuan Caterpillar bulldozer on its grid-iron lowbed as we snaked slowly through the long alpine valleys of the Alaska Highway—his feather-haired, plain-faced girlfriend was along so I had to ride curled in the sleeper in back of them, trying to keep my huge feet off their pillow, where they'd probably made love earlier—maybe he'd placed it under her hips, to raise her up to him, there was the faint musky smell which likely made the boydriver even more angry, body-angry, natural, he knew he was right to feel it—and there was a romance to their trundling drive together in the grayblack northern summer's hour-long night, a Heavy Duty Equipment romance that I'd thrown a bucket of sour radiator water on—they'd have to drive the remaining hundred miles to Fort Dawson with me lying behind their heads, a stranger they'd found stranded on a bend on Indian Head Mountain, a pathetic 'older guy' (in my late thirties) who'd actually been stupid enough to run out of gas! in the middle of noplace—I might have explained, but I didn't feel the need and there was no redemption in the teenagers' eyes—I could see that right away, they were too young to have made any of their own mistakes, they'd have that together, that very young view of the world, on how stupid 'people' were—it was relaxing in a way, that there was no forgiveness no matter what I could say and there was no way they could leave me there according to the unwritten code, stranded, but enjoying the night sky leaning back on the trunk of a #3 Fort Dawson Taxi—A taxi! on Indian Head Mountain! he'd tell his Daddy, which made me a taxi driver, the lowest on the professional driver's food chain—I could see their view on things—so I lay back looking up at the diamond-quilt roof of their coffin-like bed chamber and occasionally through the gap in the curtains out beyond the BIG RED windshield guard on the truck's nose, at the palewhite-lit road moving leftright-straight ahead, falling away and away under us—the amber strobed across the trees every few seconds like thin yellow paint swiped across the bush and needles and disappearing just as quick—the diesel sounded its driver's inherited, ancient, dark-angry, as he shifted down and down again, to just get up the grade and up the grade and finally at the top rolling easy again picking up speed shifting up, up, up, up, one gear after another then a yellow warning sign: a boxy truck pictogram heading down the next steep-graded triangle, gearing down again, gearing—he was good at it, the boydriver, probably his Daddy taught him—leading his beautiful Big Red long, hard metal and motor home safely home again—*Home!*

WHAT HAPPENED: I was at the Fort Dawson Laundromat on a Sunday late afternoon. The only other person was a gray permed change lady in powder-pink and baggy exercise pants who seemed afraid of me, maybe because I'm a bit of a giant. I've been told it's my eyes though, especially when I'm trying *not* to scare someone, they say I get a strange look and it gets worse the more I try to control it. I attempted a conversation with her, about the weather, but she looked terrified. Luckily, after a while a young guy in army fatigues came in, with real hippie beads and a faded Dead Kennedys T-shirt. He didn't want to talk either but I goaded him and he allowed that he'd just come back from *traveling around Europe* for a year. I remembered the feeling, when I got back from my same trip at his age, it was about the only time in my adult life I remembered being able to just sit back and listen, when I didn't have to talk all the time. The freedom of it lasted for a few weeks but then wore off.

When I mentioned the good weather to him he grunted and sat for a while looking right at me from the round white table by the detergent dispenser, and then out the window at the town, as if he had *disdain* for me mixed with a little intellectual sympathy, but mostly *disdain*. I could see this but I couldn't stop talking. An inner part of me stood back and watched in silence, arms folded like his, understanding all about the situation, my loneliness, my needing to talk to just about *anyone* who'd listen and how my *need*, my *needing* that, drove everyone away. I understood I was crazy to be in that town in the first place, but it was the latest in a long line of crazy decisions, that all seemed absolutely necessary at the time.

I also understood that *I had him* for an audience, I had him for as long as his clothes took to wash and dry. And I understood that the sky over the parking lot was wider than where I'd been, and I needed that and that was why I was in that pit of a town. The sky had gotten so narrow where I'd been. Whenever I looked up at the north sky, it was either the curvature of the earth, or some altering position in my head, the stretched-out blue, or black and stars made me feel better.

I was telling him about something, it didn't matter because the subject wasn't the point, he'd been staring at me for a long time with a growing glint in his eyes. He didn't fully understand his feelings towards me: *I was everything he didn't want to become.* I asked him what work he did and he said there was always good work in the north. He was originally from that same town. He said all you had to do was start a forest fire, and then get hired for good wages putting it out. A good fire might mean a whole summer's work. He said it as a challenge, to see what I would say.

Now the part of me that still understood right things from wrong, that part of me was disgusted. He was arrogant, rude and mean-spirited. He was playing a game, to see if I backbone. But I didn't let on I had any reaction at all, I couldn't risk losing his company, I just kept talking and changed the subject.

Suddenly his dryer stopped and it was quiet. I'd been talking non-stop for a long time trying to get the words out. He stuffed his clothes in his army surplus bag and walked out in holy disgust.

He'd learn.

The pink change woman had been on the payphone trying to get someone from her family to come down to save her from being alone with me. She was visibly relieved when a Ramcharger 4x4 pulled up in a sharp skid like a bulldog in the dust and a younger, pinker and blonder her came in, glaring black darts in my direction, like she knew anything about me.

My clothes were long done so I put them in my suitcase and went back up the highway towards my motel.

IN THE SAME BLOCK was the *Unisex* Hairport, I went in on a whim, it was near closing and I was sat at a chair in front of a young woman with long feathery hair like Farrah Fawcett's but darker, and she had on running shoes with a little white bobble above each heel, leaving the ankles bare. She smelled like a free perfume sample in a woman's magazine. I could tell she liked my size. She was a bit scared, but I think she liked that too.

As she started to cut we talked about the weather at first, looking at each other's reflection in the mirror when the other wasn't supposed to be looking. I told her I wanted it really short, I was job-hunting and it was a conservative town (I didn't say the last part) and short hair still helped almost anywhere, despite the sixties. I'd just gotten part-time with the local taxi while I looked. *Maybe the gas plant*, she suggested, like it was a dream come true.

As she buzzed and clipped the salon emptied of customers, mostly housewives in coloured gym pants the same as the laundry lady's. And the other hairstylers left one by one until we were alone. She was good at her job, she was slow but she knew how to move my head gently, without shoving it around like a basketball and now and then, her breasts would brush the back of my head. I didn't know if it was on purpose, or if she was just used to it from doing head after head, but gradually she started resting my head there like it was easier, holding it like that, between them, and after a while I relaxed my neck and tried to rest there. I thought I recognized Ivory Soap, and a waft of 'Charley', and I started thinking that I'd found myself more than a haircut if I wanted. Her breasts felt like home. I wanted to live in there. I wanted to live in the space between her good-sized breasts, inside her baby blue and lemon yellow expertly-knit sweater.

I moved my head just a little, pressing in a bit as if to answer her, and her hand with the needle nose scissors stopped. She rested her palm on the crown of my head.

We stayed like that for a time, neither of us meeting eyes in the mirror. It was up to me and I was trying to think of what to say or do, it'd been years since I decided there was nothing casual about casual sex for me, but I missed it real bad. I guessed we had nothing in common except our bodies' need, and of course our common humanity, I was wondering if the bad feelings afterward might outweigh the good, I was thinking too much about it as usual and I had to act! I was about to say something, anything, to stop the silence and move us forward to the next step, when suddenly the street door opened wide and one of the other hairdressers burst in, the short, large, mauve one. My hairdresser pulled away from me quickly and started clipping again fast and then some buzzing, and the other hairdresser walked slowly past us. She started humming and shifting things around in the back.

My cut was finished and I was raging like a red bull inside, but my hairdresser wouldn't look at me at all, so I paid and left. Probably she had a guy working in the woods somewhere like half of them did, her friend came back to save her from herself.

I WENT INTO THE DRYGOODS EMPORIUM next with the hairdresser's perfume still around my head, to buy the two day old newspaper up from Vancouver. The fifty-ish woman behind the cash had a sharp nose, pepper black hair and looked like she wasn't scared of me at all. It was more like she hated my guts. Her meeker business

partner was bent over wiping shelves with a J-Cloth and
a yellow and black spray gun of All Purpose Clean, she
at least looked sorry for me. The paper's front page
story was about a man kicked to death by a gang of
teenagers in Prince Rupert, a big fisherman nick-named
the 'Gentle Giant' who was walking back to his boat
from last-call.

I was about to pay when a voice spoke up from near
my elbow. It was a little guy with a pointed wispy beard,
a beat up leather hat with a floppy brim and a big smile
of broken and missing teeth, *Say, would you mind if I
bought that paper? It's the last copy.* I was going to say sorry,
but he went on, *You see I'm only in town now and then, I'm from
up in Limit and I always take a copy back to pass around. We don't
get a lot of news.*

I liked him and he kept smiling up at me, so I shrugged
and handed the paper to him and the owner woman
moved her out-held palm like a robot in his direction
instead of mine. He was the first person in the town
who'd looked me straight in the eye, it was like he had
sparks in his and he said, *Thanks, thanks a lot, mister,* like he
really meant it. *Why don't you come up to see us, any time you
like, just ask for Stig, that's me.* He said it was just up the road.

WHEN I GOT BACK to my room I turned on the satellite TV and hung my still damp jeans out on the balcony railing, it was still hot and dry and in the parking lot the dust-covered tractor trailers were lined up in the sun still high at dinner time, with their loads of thin, straight, northern trees wrapped in plastic sheet going south, or groceries, dry goods and peoples' furniture pointed north, waiting like patient dogs for their drivers in the bar next door. Nothing moved. It was that kind of town, you either went to church, or the bar, or you were alone. But I'd quit both. The church after my divorce, I was re-born just for her and the way she looked in her favourite powder blue dress. I got sucked-in for three years, the warped ideas about sex were still stuck in my head and body like a virus that wouldn't let go. It was a lot like the boozing, which was still there too, waiting, whispering in my inner ear. I'd been four years dry, but I'd lost nearly everything to the two of them.

I lay back on the bed trying not to think about the hairdresser, a movie called Scarface was on, Al Pacino yelling and throwing things. Then, before I knew it, there was this scene where they killed a guy in the shower using a chainsaw, the sound mixing with the man's screams and sudden dark blood filling the frosted enclosure. The scene only took a few seconds but I felt sick, I lunged at the set to turn it off but the snarling motor noise kept on in my head piercing and loud like deranged laughter.

I had to get out or move or something so I went and stood at the edge of the parking lot on the grass median. There were dozens of pickups angle-parked down the service roads in front of the two motel-bars and my feet took me inside the door of the closer one.

Inside it was dark at first like an old mouldy memory. I sat in a corner while my eyes adjusted and that smell of stale chemical beer. I asked the waiter if they had tea. He grimaced violently for a second like I'd told him to fuck off or go to hell, but he was used to hearing just about anything and he admitted that they had coffee, the chainsaw noise still roared in my head with the guy screaming and blood flying, I knew it would take a long time to get that out. You had to be careful what you let in. I'd been careless.

Some Indians came in, bumped hard into my table and chose the one next to mine even though there were plenty of others. They sat looking at me, not saying anything but not liking me much. It was after dinner and more Indians and whites came in and the place filled up as the sun stayed high outside the door, and after an hour I had about fifty Indians sitting all around me staring like they wanted to cut me up and throw me away in little pieces, and it finally dawned on me that I was on the Indian side. The whites stared too from their side. I was about to order forty beer all for myself when I thought of Stig's face, smiling up at me, and it gave me the power to get up and out of there.

I HAD THE KEYS to Fort Dawson Taxi #3 in my pocket, it was off-duty on slow Sunday. I walked and sort of ran to the Husky Full Serve where it sat in the rutted dirt. I wanted to see real countryside, the town was surrounded by scrubby muskeg and I wanted to drive past it into the foothills and up into the northern Rockies they'd told me started an hour from town, I wanted to see real trees and water, hills and animals, birds and flowers. I wanted to visit Stig.

Before I knew it I was hell-bent out one end of town up the Alaska Highway with my foot pressing the gas hard, #3 was a former Mountie highway cruiser, a mid-size with a fast V-8, converted to propane for cabbing.

After about an hour the ugly muskeg did end and there were real trees and brush and rocks and a stream, a real stream with little shiny rapids and then signs whipping by warning the straight was ending in a hairpin I braked and skidded and somehow stayed on the road coming out of the curve and speeding-up again into another miles-long straightaway. There were more tight curves after that and flat out again through the next mini valley and the next. I was climbing and a twisting arrow said there'd be tight turns for 25 kilometres. I slowed only as much as I had to, the road getting steeper heading up into the full mountains. My yellow knuckles clutched the wheel.

Through all this another part of me was in the back seat of the cab watching me. I saw myself yank up hard on the wheel with several manic jerks, and I heard myself screaming at the windshield, *Jesus! Jesus! Jesus!* at the top of my lungs, like some demented cowboy. I had to laugh then, but it felt good so I did it again with my head stuck out the window like a dog, *Jesus! Jesus! Jesus!* I four-wheel-drifted out of a corner, going wide approaching the next and cutting in to get the cleanest line like Richard Petty on TV and catching glimpses of snowy peaks in the distance, little tender branches in the running ditch, sun-flickering leaves and rushing currents with glinting white waterfalls. I started to climb what the government sign said was Indian Head Mountain, the road was graded and oiled dirt, baked stone-brown in the sun. I bore around another corner finally feeling more free and alive with my head wide open and straight ahead of me was the sudden squat back end of a jumbo-sized motor home with Saskatchewan prairie plates. I hit the brakes hard and skidded sideways a bit as everything came almost to a standstill pulling up behind the Winnebago trundling down the centre of the road at the speed of a jogging man. The light and sound and speed. Near stopped.

I drove behind them like that for the next while, peeking out where I could so the driver could see me in his side mirror, expecting him to let me by when he could, but he stayed where he was in the centre of the road. It was mostly tight curves one after another and mile-high cliffs. We were crawling, it felt like going backwards and I wanted rushing air and colour and movement again. I moved out more and tooted my horn, lightly, so not to spoil their rustic vacation, but it was a highway after all. But they maintained the same speed, moving in only on the curves and back out to the middle right away, even after I let off a couple of long blasts. It was tempting to pass them on the outside of a curve, there wasn't much traffic coming the other way but if there was I'd take us all over the cliff and I wasn't ready to do that. This went on for a long time, my honking with no response, just their square-butt rear end facing me and all the stuff I'd raced ahead of catching back up with me in the rear view mirror.

I could hear a faint chainsaw sound as we came around a bend near the top of the mountain and I got a clear view of the road for a couple of miles ahead, a dirt blonde strip cut into the cliff face and I saw my chance three bends ahead, a short straight, a quick S-curve and a short straight with no one coming. If I hit the top of the S right I could cut a near-straight line through, evening-out the curves. I slowed, nearly to a stop, and let the Winnebago disappear around the next bend. I waited a few more beats, counting, and then I floored the gas.

I was flying again when I rounded the corner and entered the first straight, as planned the motor home was right in front of me and I pulled wide like a stock car coming alongside before they could block me out, and some other part of me that does things I don't always understand raised my left hand out the open window with my middle finger pointing straight up to the sky, my right thumb was on the horn and my voice yelling out, *Jesus! Jesus! Jesus!* as loud as I could.

It was all in one fluid motion as I passed their front bumper and cut back in, the cliff rushing at me as I cut a perfect line through the top, middle and bottom of the S, the cliff, the road, the air.

I was through and past them and I was safe. I slowed only a little keeping on up the rest of the mountain. I knew they couldn't see me any more but I kept my finger pointing high out the window all the way to the top and starting down the other side. I laughed out loud thinking what it must have looked like: thousands of miles from a city and the taxi drivers were still crazy.

WHEN I PULLED IN at Limit, which was a highway lodge and a gas station, there was a sign that read: Last Gas for 163 K's and it hit me then that #3 ran on propane only, instead of the usual dual tank system, and it was almost on Empty. But then Stig stepped out of the cafe and smiled recognizing me.

Inside, he sat me down at the table reserved for 'staff', poured me a coffee and introduced me to his wife Mary-Lou and Harv, the old man who owned the Last Gas station next door. I felt an overwhelming relief and calm, although a little frayed at the edges. They talked and I listened, they all smiled at me and I felt like crying and that seemed okay with them, and it was such a relief for the first time in years that I had nothing much to say.

They needed to talk, they lived at the top of a mountain pass with snow at the doorstep ten months a year, five people including the two kids in the other room reading. Stig said they'd unhooked the satellite dish, they'd had TV for six months but everyone had started to fight over what to watch. One evening Mary-Lou got out the pliers, went outside and cut through the wire. *It's better to own your own head*, she said, nodding to herself. She was the kind of person who rocked a little while she sat. Harv nodded too but wasn't as sure, for just a second he looked like a dog just finished breakfast and longing for dinner, but then he lit his pipe and settled back into a more comfortable place in his mind. They talked about the black bear Stig had killed, it was the only time his face clouded. A man from Hamburg had walked right in for a close-up and the bear killed him with his family watching from the rented camper. Stig did a little outfitting and it was in his area so they called on him to do the bear. *I'd rather shoot the tourist*, was all he said. His name had been in the Fort Dawson paper which seemed to alarm him. Maybe he had a past life too and didn't want it to find him.

I told them I'd once met a man from Germany, he'd told me that where he came from 'Canada' meant a huge, empty space. Like if you were in Bavaria and you walked into a big, vacant field you might say, *Scheisse, it's Canada man!* Out the window the motor home rounded the bend, drove by slowly and was gone into the sun that had finally come down nearer to the jagged white mountain rim. But the tanks strapped to its back reminded me about the propane and I asked Harv if he had it. He didn't and I tried to explain that taxis usually ran on gas too, they were nice about it but didn't have a solution and I decided to try and not think about it until later. I looked at Stig, he wasn't smiling any more. He was asking me a question without saying it, his eyes saying, *Are you O.K.?* He looked a signal to Mary-Lou and Harv and said to me, *Wanna go for a ride?* and I realized it was that old look they could see in my eyes. I shrugged and got up, my legs suddenly shaky, and I followed Stig out the back door.

STIG TOOK ME UP A STEEP ROAD that he said led to a radar station high on one of the snow covered peaks all around. We drove for a long time in the half-light, not saying anything, slow and steady and higher, far from the skinny line highway below. I realized, for the first time, that most of the wilderness had nothing to do with the highway or the towns. I'd seen it through glass windows my whole life, but for a thousand miles in all directions there were almost no people.

Stig's surplus Jeep was having trouble with a steep part, leaning hard to my side as the left front wheel lifted like a leg over a large boulder that made up half the road and then the rear wheel too, up, there was no door and I held on to the seat cushion looking down into the pass below, but I noticed near my elbow there were tiny blood-red flowers springing from cracks in the rocks and suddenly we were over the rise, leveled and stopped in the slanted sun on a high plateau.

Stig cut the motor. It was quiet in the wind moving in the rippling grass and the blossoms and the front of my shirt. Stretching away from our feet the wide meadow was covered in grazing big horn sheep, their huge heads lowered in the shadowgreen. I stood on a knot of rock and dirt that was higher than the rest and spread my arms out to take it in, trying to be a part of it. *Jesus! Jesus! Jesus!* I heard myself yell. The sun shifted and the light altered. Stig coughed and looked at me like he knew all about it, as my little voice echoed brokenly off the blunt rock face and got lost in the valleys below.

3 GREENS

124

1

green salt chuck

Rick's Dad

had an aluminum car-topper with *Tyee Princess* hand-painted on the bow and a shining black 9.8 outboard he bought at the Mercury Marine. They'd troll back and forth across the bay at dawn looking for that secret big hungry school of fish hidden deep under the slow-heaving surface of the milk-green chuck. Rain or shine they'd dress right in layers in winter, gut-stained floater jackets and Mom's hand-knit zip-up sweaters with soaring ducks and fish leaping from the their chests and backs, sitting hunched over, steaming from their mouths.

They had little bells tied to the ends of their rods. The idea was to relax, the bells would tinkle lightly in the wind, or with the boat's rock. But there were fewer and fewer fish. Even so, some days a rod would suddenly dip hard and steep down at the water's edge, the bell jangling hard, upset, and they'd sit straight and grab whoever's rod it was, pull it out of the holder, prop a foot against the thin metal gunwale and hold on tight.

His Dad taught him how to do it: first thing was the dial on the slack adjuster—too loose and they'd run away with the line, too tight they might break away with a quick jerk—depending on the strength and smarts of the unseen fish. As they dove deep, or surfaced to dance on their tails trying to shake free of the barbed hook ripping at their mouths they would slowly tire and you could start reeling in, turning the slack depending on what the fish was doing—not too soon, letting it tire out. If they were big you might not reel-in at all for half an hour. Just hold on. The rod between your knees.

Holding the rod with a fish fighting the other end of the line felt good. Especially to think of eating it fresh that night.

But the last year they hadn't caught a thing, his Dad always said it didn't matter, they were going fishing and might or might not catch a fish, it was second, to going fishing. His Mom and sisters didn't understand, when they got home they always asked if they caught anything, right away. Rick's Dad would frown his shadow face and head for the TV, Rick knew, if they caught something they'd obviously be holding it in front of them.

There were no more fish and his Dad was angry all the time. Especially when the Canucks lost. Rick was beginning to realize his Dad always seemed angry except when he was fishing, away from the house, away from Mom. It was the year the mill went to one shift that his Dad started yelling at her. Rick was afraid he'd hit her so he stood between them, she'd told him he was man in the house when his Dad was away, 'looking for work', which was more often than not. One time his Dad threw a kitchen chair against the sliding door but it bounced off stupidly clattering on the floor and he left for three weeks then.

Rick's Dad was more and more away, the house breathing easier when he was gone. But Rick always knew if he was back—when he got home from school, before he saw anyone, the black acid rain cloud hanging in the air. Rick would be between them again, listening for the bell to ring to start another round. Stepping in the front door was being on the wrong end of the line, being pulled into a place where he couldn't breath, life pulling, pulling him.

2

green horn

Carl just twenty-one

arrived in a puny oil-can town south of the Arctic Circle. He shivered with the flu, wanted to go to bed, dizzy on his feet as he entered the tiny hotel lobby to meet Arnold, the older man sent to pick him up. The introductions went on, the hotel clerk, two other male forms, all was quiet and he could lie down soon.

Then the air changed as the padded door from the bar bedlam next door slammed open and a towering three-hundred-pound woman in an expanse of gray thermal undershirt and giant jeans burst through, she had rock heavy steps and laughed in a booming voice like a bear in a dream. She stopped in her tracks when she saw Carl, taking in his body like he was a cornered rodent-morsel, she lumbered drunk-jolly to him until she stood an inch from him, blocking out the bare bulb sun and staring straight down into his face.

The room spun beside him but her dark weight was all he could see, he watched as her hand swung back, came in, and she grabbed him by the balls, squeezing them hard.

She talked in a low growling curse, *Hey, you're cute. How'd you like to come with me...* she paused, dropping to a rattler-hiss, *...and I'll fuck ya 'til your balls drop off!?* She was all wild grin filling everything, her fingers still holding him tight.

She turned sideways to Arnold, the deskman, from laughing manshadow to manshadow. Carl was trying not to throw up, the room rearing as the bear ripped at the insides of his head. He muttered slow and meek, *I've-got-the-flu.*

It was quiet, but she didn't let go. So Carl took her wrist, and squeezed as hard as he could for a long time, until finally she loosened her grip and he moved her hand away, guiding it carefully from his sore sack. In her eyes she looked alarmed for just a second, but then she shrugged her shoulder mounds, smiled gentle and quick so no one else saw and shrank to human for just a second and then back up to bear. Stepping back and winking at the other men she laughed and roared, *Oh... the shy type, eh?* and she spun through the double doors back into the blinding smoke and noise.

The other men looked around the room, anywhere but at Carl. Arnold sighed and looked ashamed as he picked up Carl's bag and took him out to the truck.

3

red-light-green

Seamus Twain drove

his Dodge RAM tow-truck in aimless circuits around the Toronto downtown, taking long drinks from a new bottle of Canadian Club, looking out at the neons, the anonymous crowd, the long legged women with their men in rich sweaters. He was seventeen and fresh from the north scrag beyond Thunder Bay. He was in charge of his truck, he did his job and no one told him what to do besides.

Each night he memorized the best body parts of the women he saw, and if he couldn't wait 'til he got home he'd masturbate into the toilet bowl at a gas station.

In Little Portugal he idled at a red light beside three old people arguing on the sidewalk: a couple, owners of a small grocery, him bald and stocky, her plump and olive-faced holding his arm, holding him back. The third was a woman, an old scarecrow with straight white, dead hair like straw, one arm wrapped across the front of her body and the other reaching out, grabbing food from the stand and stuffing it into her mouth. The man in the white apron was yelling at her, getting more and more red face pissed off, grabbing her arm and pushing her away. But she kept stepping in, grabbing more food and stuffing it in her mouth, just a few crumbs getting in and most of it falling on the ground.

She yelled back, *Gimme-I just want-gimme-something god-damned to eat!* He was starting to get violent, pushing harder, his wife holding his arm, pulling him back, hard. He wanted to hit the old lady. She wouldn't stop.

The grocer suddenly looked over at Seamus idling at the curb, he looked ashamed but it was just a shadow sliding across his face without stopping mixed with the anger and then the old woman broke away, turning to face the street. A group of suburban teenagers left the Home Burgers next door, laughing and dancing around each other like models, until they saw her, their thin voices stopping, one by one.

She staggered one step at a time towards Seamus in his truck, as she came closer he saw there were prune-coloured welts hanging below her eyes—and as she stopped outside his open window, her arm fell away from her chest. She'd been holding her faded flower shirt closed. It had no buttons and it opened wide. Her bare breasts, they were small, shrunken and flat, her skin was chalk-white.

The light turned green and Seamus gunned his truck across the street.

GORDON'S
HEAD

The 7-11:

I'm fishing in my pocket for money, checking out a girl's skin-tight jeans bending over Ninja Voodoo Warriors, the joy stick moving nervously in her hand. Sun on gritty pavement out the window, bright streaming cars, an empty space where my bicycle had been, *Fuck, No!*

I'm suddenly outside, running to the curb looking up and down the street. No one's riding a bicycle, people, *Did you see? My bike's been stolen. There. Against the window.* Blank stares, someone, a woman, *Yes, I saw a man get on a bicycle. He rode up the street just a minute ago.*

RUNNING up the street, yelling, grunting back, *Thanks! ... Shit ...*

I'VE GOT THIS BROTHER, Gordon, that I haven't seen since, elementary school. I hardly even think of him for months at a time, but I guess he's always in the back of my head somewhere. I've always been, afraid, that I couldn't take things like he couldn't.

Gordon had a stroke a few years ago they told me, which is pretty unusual for someone in their twenties they say. So now they figure it was something physical in him all along, that they just don't know much about.

But I don't see the difference. I mean, they say there's all these chemicals in us, in our brains, that are *released* from somewhere to somewhere else, and we've only got so much control over that.

Sometimes, I think Gordon just saw things the way they are, crazy, I mean, with all these people running around trying to keep themselves distracted. Like all these movies and shows, rushing out, and sitting, and being distracted. From what? Our own thoughts? At home with the TV on or always with the radio on, trying to keep those thoughts a little, off balance. And maybe Gordon couldn't do that. And I guess, or I tell myself, that I don't want to.

But it's how most people, the ones I see anyway, seem to survive. Always one step ahead of seeing anything like it is. And he saw things like they are, and that put him in a whole different world from almost anyone else. So people, along with everything else, saw this alien, and they were afraid of him. So they did all they could to make his life shit. Maybe to distract him too.

Now I haven't seen him in a long time, and I'm feeling guilty like I always do when I think about him. Scared too. I guess I'm always walking around with these thoughts in the back of my head, but I'm just too distracted to notice them.

I wonder if he'd recognize his kid brother, because he doesn't hardly anyone. The last time I saw him, I thought it was strange, the way he looked at me, and at my new bike.

And now he lives in Vancouver, and I guess if I went there I'd probably forget all about him, being distracted and all, until after I left.

HEY GORDON, COME ON OUTSIDE. I wanna show you my new bike. It's got ten speeds.

I hadn't seen him in months. He was staying at some kind of psychiatric halfway house, he couldn't live with us any more. This was after he'd gone to the Eric Martin Institute a couple of times. I remember the kids at school used to make fun of the people in Eric Martin, sticking their tongues out and rolling their eyes.

He'd been in there, but I don't think on the sixth floor with the barred windows.

I was excited about my new bicycle. My old one had been stolen and there were these fancy new ten speeds, and I had one. He was standing way above me. I think he asked if he could try it. He was so big, and strange. And dangerous? I think I must have said no, or he read it in my eyes. 'Cause afterwards, looking down at me with those eyes, not quite dead like later, they said the bicycle was doing something to him, inside.

I realized that day, at the back of the carport, that people liked me and that they didn't like him. That I was scared of him. That I didn't like him coming around any more. 'Cause he made Mom feel bad, and he made my new bicycle something bad.

WHEN I WAS LITTLE, I used to love this show on TV called *J.P.Patches*, it was about a poor clown that lived in the town dump. One of my favourite things was when he'd go to this empty television set he had at the back of his shack. He'd squat down in front of it and he'd look right through at you from where the picture tube had been. He'd twiddle the knobs and the dials, and then he'd say, *Let's see. Whose birthday is it today? Oh yes. Gordon. Gordon is twenty-six today. Gordon, go look in the dryer.* And you could picture this kid named Gordon running down the stairs to look in the dryer for his present.

And every time J.P. would have a visitor he'd walk to the half-door at the back of his shack, and he'd wave good-bye. Then he'd turn around and walk slowly back in, start talking about something else... then he'd remember, he'd run back to the door and say, *Hey, watch out for the hole!* and just then you heard this, *AHHHHHHHHHHHHhhhhhhhhhh...!* and every time, you'd be jumping up and down as the guy left, saying, *Tell them about the hole! Tell them about the hole!*

GORDON USED TO TELL US STORIES, me and Richard in the kitchen beside Mom's crazy bulletin board with all her clippings and sayings. He'd say, *Give me any subject, just any*. It was usually about racing car drivers. On and on the story would turn and twist and build and build, and we'd sit forward with our eyes lit up. And there'd be this big ending. And he made it all up as he went along. Especially Richard, would have his mouth open wide and he'd clap. Richard didn't have a bigger brother.

Richard's my only friend who knew about Gordon. Others would find out I had a, missing, bigger brother. Mom said to just say he'd gone away and to leave it vague. But Christ, you learned not to talk to her about it. She'd curl up in a ball on the sofa, and with those eyes. She thought about him all the time anyway.

I think the psychiatrists told her that everything was *your environment* then, which meant that it was my parents' fault. Or my Mom thought so anyway. Or tried not to. I'd sure like to kick their asses. But maybe they were just trying to figure all this stuff out. But Christ, this guy with a beard and glasses in our living room asking us questions.

Gordon had had a stroke, in the Riverview Mental Hospital in Vancouver. My mother, even standing looking like she was curled in a ball on the couch beside the net curtains. I remember her telling me secretly then, that she couldn't help feeling glad, no matter what that meant, for the proof that it was something physical in him all along. Because you don't usually have a stroke in your twenties. But the pain for her to say that, to herself as much as me. I guess she must have trusted me a lot to say it.

I ALWAYS SEEM TO TALK about Gordon in the past tense. I haven't seen him in a long time. They say he doesn't recognize hardly anyone but that it's good for the nurses to see he's had a visitor. Even Richard made jokes about Eric Martin crazy people. Everyone did. Even I wanted to sometimes.

Al's big brother told him about Gordon. Al and I were enemies at the time, for some reason. He told Dave and Blair that my brother was some kind of lunatic stupid jerk. I guess Al's brother was one of the people pushing Gordon in the halls, chasing him home after school, pointing. I guess he told Al about certain jerk things my brother did. Like every school has two or three kids that are tortured by everyone else, because they dress funny, or maybe you find out later they were gay, or something else. Or maybe you just don't know how it got started but it's like a snowball and it does stuff to them that they'll never get over.

HEY GORDON, *come on outside. I wanna show you my new bike. It's got ten speeds.* He didn't say anything. *See. You push this lever here and the gear changer moves down there.* He didn't say anything. Neither did I. Then he said, *That's... great. Can I try it?* I didn't say anything. Neither did he.

THERE WAS A FIGHT going on in the schoolyard. Gordon was handsome, with a strong sensitive face, like an actor's, dark hair, and he ended up big too, six-foot-four, and broad. But if there was ever a person with not much aggression in him it was him. I was seven years old, St. Patrick's Elementary, and the usual yell that goes up with a fight. And there's this kid, same age as Gordon, maybe a foot shorter, not that strong or anything, he's hitting Gordon in the face, then he's turning to the crowd, he's joking, he's turning back and he's hitting him in the stomach. They're laughing. Gordon's got a cut on his face, but it isn't anything 'cause it's his eyes, totally confused that this could happen to anyone, let alone him. That all these people, and he's so funny 'cause he's so big. And they love it. The spectacle of my big brother.

I guess I must have been embarrassed to be his brother, 'cause I must have left. I mean I was too little to stop it or anything.

I WAS IN THE KITCHEN I think, he came home and like usual, he was in high school then, he went upstairs. He had a record player and all the Beatles' albums and this was maybe the most important thing in his life.

After he'd been upstairs for a few seconds, he yelled. This long deep yell in his huge voice, that I don't want to remember now but I do. Mom came out from somewhere. I was looking upstairs. His closed door. There were crashing footsteps and yelling. He flew open his door and came towering down the stairs, out the swinging-banging front door, the police found him a few days later near Port Alberni sleeping in a barn.

Mom went upstairs first, all in pain. He'd left his Beatles' albums spread out across his bed and the sunlight had been pouring in on them all day. They were warped completely out of shape, so he'd smashed them all, and torn up the jackets. Half of Paul McCartney's face.

IT WAS THE LAST DAY OF SCHOOL. We had these huge Safeway bags full of popcorn and these big bottles of pop. And Andy McCormick was this little kid, I mean we were all little, but he was this sad kid in that people would gang up maybe twenty or more and chase him home yelling. And he'd have these terrible eyes, I mean fucking scared.

I guess I must have gone along on my bike too, 'cause I wouldn't remember this stuff otherwise.

But Andy must have said something to me that day with all the popcorn, calling me a name loud and the whole class turning. It was something he figured he could say to me 'cause I was on the edge of all the groups, semi-accepted by all of them, but not too much a part of any one so not too dangerous.

So I took an empty pop bottle into the hall and filled it at the fountain. When I came back Andy was at the front of the class still trying to get everyone's attention, and for a moment he started to have it, 'cause everyone started looking as I was sneaking up behind him. And I guess he must have thought everyone was smiling at whatever it was he was saying.

So I had the bottle of water in my hand and I was sneaking up behind him, and he was really excited, waving his arms, yelling. Finally, I was right behind him, and everyone was looking at me, not him. I lifted the bottle of water high above his head and magically he still didn't turn around. I tilted the bottle, and all the water started to pour out and down and onto and all over him, all over his head, splashing onto his shoulders, down his back. They were screaming with delight. And Andy didn't move. He just stood there absolutely still, with all the water pouring out, splashing onto him, his hair slicked flat against his head, it all just running down, these big bubbles one after another, rising and breaking. And he didn't move.

And I was some kind of hero, for doing that I guess. I don't even remember what happened after. I guess I must have been happy, and I guess he must have been sad. I don't really remember.

MAYBE I HAVEN'T GONE TO SEE GORDON in all this time for another reason, than the one I've used for a long time— that being, that I was, am, scared, that I'm so much like him and I've never been sure that I could take things like he couldn't. And that somehow he'd be contagious.

Like I said, I don't think of him that much.

But maybe, it's just that I don't like him. Like Andy McCormick was him. Maybe Andy didn't call me a name that day but was just acting weird.

Gordon scared me, and my family. Maybe I just didn't like anything about him after a while.

He was weak.

But how the Hell did he end up in there and not me? I guess I didn't like him along with everyone else. People have always liked me.

It wasn't that he was so big, and clumsy. I mean, sure I thought he'd break my bike—but on purpose.

I should've let him ride it though.

... BLANK STARES, someone, a woman, *Yes, I saw a man get on a bicycle. He rode up the street just a minute ago.*

RUNNING up the street, yelling, grunting back, *Thanks! Shit*, slight hill, running so fast, in my stomach words gripping it hard saying: don't bother—no hope—gone. But three already stolen. No number four!

Running to the corner around the backs and fronts of stopped cars at a red light. Stopping, looking across the intersection and way across the park, through the far trees. There!

Running across the street, cars braking, side-step, dodging them. Still see him. Running-straight-line-open-field pumping, face hard with adrenaline.

He's following the bike path up there in there between the trees, taking his time. Police car following me on the roadway beside the grass, *Hey, buddy, where's the fire?* Still running, pointing, *That bastard's stealing my bike!* Running hard. Hear Police engine racing away, has to follow winding park road to ahead beyond the trees— to cut him off?

I'm in spaced trees now, almost completely straight line, closer, gaining ground, insane speed seems for a human being, need my goddamn bicycle get him BASTARD for the others too! My heart starting to hurt a bit, too many goddamned cigarettes NOT slowing keep pumping, six, seven more trees, bike lane curving, he doesn't see me coming in straight line across grass and pine needles, bike path and road and me coming together TWO MORE TREES he's slowing, he's looking each way before crossing the road, he glances back over his shoulder at me coming mad insane running flailing bullet straight line to target. He's pumping hard once, twice, again hard, to get away and just stay beyond my reaching, glancing back at me again, neither of us seeing blue and white POLICE tires screeching as he rides right in front of it KNOCKED—HIT over rolls once, again. His head pathetically breaking on the curb. Bones, skin. My bike mangled. My foot going back to kick the writhing thing on the ground. *Hey!*

He looks like my brother.

(From the 16mm film: Gordon's Head , ©1993 Cyclops Productions)

HITLER!

a filmpoem

HITLER!

my brother yells at the teenage
girls jig / dancing at the front of
the room. The big jolly nurse,
looming over Niall to wish him /
a Merry Christmas, grins, *That's
what he calls me each / morning.
Don't take it personal,* I say.

The dancers, they're wearing red kilts holding their arms / up high and pointing their toes at the floor, their thighs / flash white as their dresses lift up and twirl. They have / that far-away look, like small caught animals have. / I don't know where to look myself.

Each time they spin, the girls' skirts open up, flowers / blooming, their long, straight legs like stamens in the wind. / It's weird the way they seem so unaware of it, / with their aggressive white-toothed smiles, teeth clenched like / synchronized swimmers.

They disappear, and come back in polyester / sailor suits, the song from Popeye the Sailor Man / starts playing from their boom box, but with a disco / beat. Their hands hold invisible oars out in front / of them, their elbows and knees bend out to their sides.

When I started the visits, at first it was hard / to see past the waving arms and kicking legs, to / see who was really there, and the dancers, they can't. / The sailor number's at its peak now. They're spinning / fasterandfaster to-the-beat like dervishes / up on their toes.

And Niall's raising his arm straight up and out at / them now, fingers pressed together, at first I think / he wants something. But the nurse says to me, *That's a / Hitler-style salute.* Then she leans in close, nodding / towards the girls, *They look very well bred don't they?*

They row. Their eyes straight ahead. Their long legs open / and close, I can barely watch them. They really do / scare me. I realize that I'm staring at him, / I try to see past his missing teeth, chocolate / and spit on his chin, and he's smiling at me now, / he knows who I am, his little brother, he likes me / he doesn't hate me.

His smile isn't any stranger than the dancers' / just more rare, you'll never see it on TV ads. / *Yoko Ono*, he says, two more of his words, then, / *Hamburger, gift.* I ask him if I should bring him / a hamburger for a gift next time, but he turns / his head down to his lap, looking sad all of a / sudden, the way he does.

He says, low so I can barely hear it, *Ya, ya.* / That's a new word as far as I know, it's the first / time he's ever answered one of my questions, straight.

One day he yelled at me,
at the top of his lungs, /
FUCKING   ASS   HOLE!
right in my face.

That was the worst visit, it made me feel like a / weak, little kid. When I was five years old he talked / me into touching the new electric hot plate. / He said it was okay, because it was black not / red. I burned my hand badly and he laughed and laughed.

I'm still scared of Niall

but I'm trying to look /
right at him, inside him,

                                        inside me too.

HITLER!
he yells.

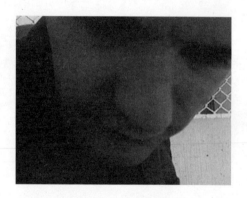

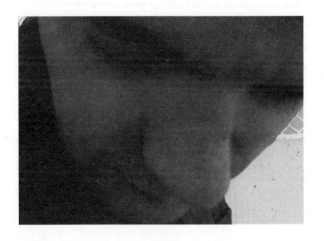

(From the 16mm film: Hitler!, ©1995 Cyclops Productions)

About the author:

CLIVE HOLDEN writes fiction and poetry and has made two experimental films, *Gordon's Head* and *Hitler!*, both of which are about his relationship with his schizophrenic brother, Niall.

At the time of this printing, Clive Holden is completing the first titles in a line of literary audio CDs, featuring various authors, to be published by Cyclops Press. They will be available in stores, and for direct purchase, along with the CD *Gordon's Head & Hitler!—experimental film soundtracks*, at: www.cyclopspress.com.